VERITAS FILES (Book 1)

THE GIFTED

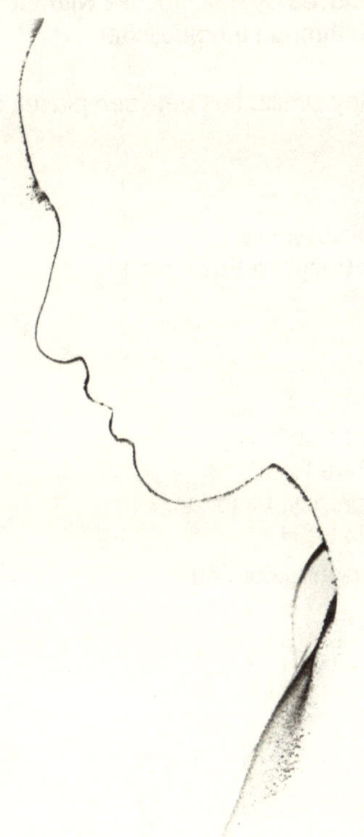

Pamela Dabbs

First published by Busybird Publishing 2020

ISBN
978-1-922465-30-6 (paperback)
978-1-922465-31-3 (ebook)

Cover design: Busybird Publishing
Layout and typesetting: Busybird Publishing

Busybird Publishing
2/118 Para Road
Montmorency, Victoria
Australia 3094
www.busybird.com.au

To those who encouraged, did not laugh when I said I was writing a book. Who congratulated me and supported me. You know who you are. Thank You

Contents

Chapter 1

Terra Hope

A sudden jerk forward as the bus comes to another stop. As my eyes open, I quickly realise, it's my stop. Half asleep still I jump out of my seat and grab my bag from the overhead feeling a little embarrassed with all the banging and clattering I am doing. Moving quickly and clumsily I make my way to the front of the bus, not even looking to see if I left anything behind as I get off. I wait for my bag out of the luggage hold and think to myself another new start in another new place. This is number seventeen.

Terra Hope is a beautiful coastal town with palm trees and of course my one true place of serenity, the beautiful ocean. Reams of ink black, deep purple and silver shimmer in the moonlight. I don't know why but I am drawn to the ocean— the sound of the surf, the salty air— and how calm it makes me feel. Which for me is a godsend. It's been my go-to place for the last eighteen months where I feel calm, especially considering the world I come from.

I have been travelling on this bus for the last sixteen hours and experienced an acknowledgement at each of the thirteen stops. Each stop everyone jerks forward in their seats, the poor old lady in the seat opposite lost her false teeth three stops ago. The bus driver 'Jerry' late fifties, heavy really heavy, balding and wearing those old seventies silver-rimmed glasses with lenses that say without these on he is blind, they make his eyes look so big. It does make me ask myself how on earth he got a licence to drive this bus! I bet his weight is from too many fast food choices rather than watching what he eats, but is the type of person who professes its 'glandular'. Every young women entering the bus gets one of 'those' stares that make you very uncomfortable, you know that he is undressing you with great delight. Such a perv! But makes a point of introducing himself, welcoming you onto his bus. "Hi I'm Jerry your driver today." The name badge on his grey shirt that should really be white and has seen better days is the giveaway of his name.

"Jerry," the bus driver of the year!

But I am sure the way he drives is for his own entertainment. Every stop I was thrown forward in my seat, noticing his eyes in the rear-view mirror and smirking to himself. I told myself there was no way I was going to sleep. Luckily the distance between the last two stops was about fifty minutes so I did manage to get some sleep. Unfortunately it was tormented by thoughts of Duke and the Veritas Team at Dukes place.

Jerry has managed to prise himself out of his seat to open the luggage hold. Panting and sweating from the few steps he has taken out of the bus. I grab my trusty rucksack, the two bags hold everything I own in this world. Plus, over my shoulder is my only extravagance— a Louis Vuitton bumbag. It always stays close to my heart. Inside a picture of my parents, my

Veritas ID card and about five thousand dollars in cash all small used bills.

I have arrived late into Terra Hope, its 11pm. Its dark but I try to take in as much of the scenery as I can, while behind me the bus drives off on its way to the next stop. I have my large rucksack on my back and my Camo Bag as always at the front of me. Wow it's so beautiful I think to myself, this is definitely going to be it, I think to myself. I close my eyes and take a deep calming breath. As I open my eyes, it floods back why I am here.

Three weeks ago, I was so happy. I was in the Helen Town Peninsula. Quite a bustling town by the sea of course! But with a village or rural feel to it. The place where everyone knows everyone's business kinda town.

I was living in a small bedsit sharing a house with three others. Triplets Jamie, Julie and Jarrod. The three J's who would look at each other and pretend they were telepathic. No surprise, it took them a while to rent out their spare room. I think you need to be some kind of weird to understand them or at least be able to live with it. But for me I found it normal based on everything I have lived with over the last eighteen years, so I put myself in the weird category. I knew they were only pretending to be telepathic. It takes a gifted to recognise another gifted. Although, twins and triplets etc do have some form of sixth sense between them it's a common trait in multiple births. That's something the Institute relied upon.

The house itself was quite big but my little room on the ground floor had the greatest view. Big old metal French doors leading to a small deck that looked out over the beach. I would spend every moment I could sitting out on the deck and watching the tide move in and out, listening to the surf crash against the shore. Which of course was not as often as

I would like due to working at Café Verona. Plus, a bonus factor is its locality was only a block from the bus or train station ready for a quick departure if needed.

Every place I stay at I pray this is the last one hoping to be free.

I had the most amazing job at Café Verona. I was just waiting staff, but Duke he looked after me like a daughter. It was a family run business owned by Duke, a real kind and generous man who really looked out for me.

Duke's real name was Barry but after a trip to Hawaii and Waikiki Beach he loved the story of Duke Kahanamoku and saw so many similarities of his own life and that of the Duke, he saw himself as the new Duke or at least an Australian version, and it just stuck. His wife Helena would tease him about it at every BBQ and family gathering. What was so special was how I was included all the time, they made me part of their family and I loved it.

My last memories of Duke are haunted by pain and suffering. As usual my shift at Café Verona started at 6.45am on the dot. I arrived as always fifteen minutes before my shift began. I like to be early and Duke was always in before me. It was always just me and Duke setting up before the cafe opened at 9am. He was always so kind he knew I needed the money and would give me as many hours as I could manage.

As I walked into the kitchen tying my apron around my waist and just as I was about to shout out "Morning Duke," I stopped suddenly as I heard raised voices in the main dining area. I felt cold, that sinking feeling in the pit of my stomach – an all too familiar a feeling. I froze and as I looked around the kitchen, I realised it's a mess. There are broken plates, cutlery and glass all over the floor, the dishwasher door is open with steam rising and… oh no! I can see blood on the floor. Fear is rising, I begin to shake, and my heart is beating so fast- it feels like it will burst out of my chest. I feel sick and want to throw up. I have tears welling up in my eyes and I just know…

They are here!

Carefully stepping towards the main dining area, trying to avoid anything that may raise attention to me. There is a gap between the double doors that separate the kitchen from the main dining area. From here I knew I could see what was going on without being seen myself. The voices were getting louder in the main dining area as I reached the doors. Slowly turning my head to look through the gap, trying to slow down my breathing that was so erratic and full of panic as I told myself this will give me away. Duke is taped to a chair, there are three big guys all standing over him. They look like army types all in black trouser tucked into their boots like the army wear with back t -shirts that look painted on. It's amazing how far lycra stretches I thought to myself. It's the same team I saw at Ruby Hills.

I could see that Duke is bleeding- I shudder as I realise he has been tortured. Duke is a good man and he does not deserve this. I knew I had to do something, As I put my hand up to the door to push open I saw him, a fourth man. I recognised him, the grey hair and black rimmed square glasses, he was there before in Lake Willow, Ruby Hills and now here. He works for General Page. I stoped moving but asked myself, how can I help Duke, what do I do now? All the questions running through my mind.

The Panic is rising now through my whole body and I remember the feeling of being frozen on the spot. I can't go in and save Duke I told myself as they will take me back or worse, It's time to go, but then I remember thinking what about Duke he never knew. This man suddenly shouts again to Duke, "Where is she?" scaring me out of my thoughts. Duke just looks up at him and says, "I don't know who you are talking about." The grey-haired man gestures to one of the muscle guys with an upturn of his head and I saw a smashing right hook hit Duke and his head flop down resting his chin on his chest, he's out cold. Poor Duke how can I save him from this is all I could think at the time. I knew I had to run and I had to do it now with no time to waste but this man has been so good to me for the last eight and a half months he deserves my help. Even though he won't know it's me.

I have panic surging through my whole body and conflict as I want to rush in there and save Duke just as he saved me with his kindness.

There was no doubt in my mind these men are from Veritas. I needed to move and move quickly as I try to calm myself and really think of whats the next move to make. I realised what I needed to to and I turned and begin weaving my way back through all the mess on the kitchen floor, carefully making sure I make no sound to alert them. I picked up the kitchen phone and checked for a dial tone. Yes, thank god I think to myself and dial 000. I gave the address and said there are men with guns come quickly. I don't hang up but put the phone on the kitchen countertop ensuring the line is open.

I leave through the back door the way that I had came in. Then quickly start to run back to my bedsit, luckily only a short run from the cafe. But my feet felt like lead weights I had tears streaming down my face, that began the moment I heard the commotion and never stopped. It was only about a tenminute walk to the café from the bedsit and luckily only a quick fiveminute run. The relief as I reach the door, my trusted blue door.

My hands were shaking with fear I think at the time it must be all the adrenalin, perhaps a little bit of both. As I reached for my keys in my pocket and unlocked the door, I felt some relief as this did feel like home. I just grabbed all my clothes off their hangers and out of the draws stuffing them into my rucksack, then gathering everything else into the Camo Sack. I stopped for a moment to breathe and recall leaning against the wall by the door, the same feelings rising of panic, plus confusion and real sadness that again they have found me, and I needed to run. I had hoped this would be my sanctuary and fresh start.

I knew this had been the longest stay anywhere since I first began to settle in various new places. But I can't help wondering How do they find me? I tell myself that I am careful; use only cash, change my name and identity every new place. As I wonder to myself , what am I doing that leads them to me? Having managed eight and a half months here. Making the last memory of this wonderful place by taking a last look around, taking a deep breath and by closing my eyes to calm myself then making the move to leave, taking in all the last moments in this wonderful place. My racing heart and mind are distracted as I recall at that point hearing police sirens approaching and suddenly, As I opened my eyes, I realised that I am calm and now determined, as this is the distraction, I think that I need to get away.

I grab my bags and taking one last look turn and head out of the door.

I had my plan in place and headed towards the bus station, it's in the opposite direction to the café and only a block from the house. As I began the walk, I hear the sound of sirens getting louder. I sighed in relief as this tells me they are closing fast thinking of Duke that he is about to be saved, then of course, it made me realise that I was out in the open and the Veritas Team trying to find me will hear the sirens and leave the café.

My pace quickens almost to a run, As I can see the bus station and just keep my focus ahead of me.

I entered the bus station and looked around surveying the people in there, who are these people I asked myself, is there anyone that is looking for me I wondered? Tried but could not sense any gifted here, which tells me it was safe. So, after locating the departure screens my first check was, what is the next bus leaving the station? I scanned quickly, then I saw it, on the regional transit terminal only three minutes for a departure to Terra Hope. I rushed over to the ticket machine and of course with the day I am having it's not working. The queue to the attendant is five deep I would never make the bus in time. I spotted an older man who looked like he worked there, well he is in uniform I thought to myself. Probably late fifties early sixties. Crisps white hair and blue eyes that remind me of the sea. By making eye contact I hoped he would be the one to help and he smiled asking, "Can I help you miss?"

"if you could please," I replied. I explained I needed to get on the next bus to Terra Hope, pointing at the departure screens, explaining my grandfather is very ill and if I don't get this bus I am not sure that I will make it in time He looked at me and could see I had been crying and was still upset but of course not knowing the real reason I believe he took pity but showed real kindness.

He said, "Don't worry miss I will get you all sorted out, it's gonna be ok." He went to the attendants booth and put me at the front of the queue, Much to the disapproval of the people waiting. He turned and smiled and said, "you'll be ok now." It felt so reassuring and as I smiled back at him. thanking him as I start to head out of the terminal to the departure area.

Ticket in hand I ran out to the bus. The driver, "Jerry" just tutted at me looking at his watch and then he stood watching me as I threw my bag into the luggage hold. I didn't pay any attention to him waved my ticket at him and got onto the bus. He then closed the luggage doors and clambered into the bus.

This was the final check as I stopped for a moment closed my eyes and calming my heartbeat and breathing I scanned the bus for any gifted. It was clear! When I open my eyes and looked for an available seat. I saw three rows from the back on the driver's side, the driver shouts from his seat to take your seat please and begins to pull away from the terminal. I quickly took my seat. Putting a bag in the overhead and slide over to the window still looking all around checking for the Veritas Team.

Nothing!

The bus heads out in the direction of Café Verona, The hairs on the back of my neck were standing upright as I saw flashing blue lights from the police cars that are blinding as we get closer. I saw a few people gathering looking to each other and trying to see what was going on. An ambulance was there, and I just saw a glimpse of Duke coming out on a stretcher, relief, thank God he will be ok now I tell myself. Just seeing that made me cry again, I sobbed into my hands but trying not to make any noise or any attention to myself but the old lady sitting across from me offers me a tissue saying, "There dear are you alright?."

I took the tissue and gave her a smile for her kindness and nod to her to answer her question. I turned to look out of the window and spotted the Veritas Team getting into a G wagon. Black, tinted windows the works. I think to myself do all spies, mercenaries and government agencies go to the same car dealers- Pimpedoutspyride.com. One size, colour suits all!

As I slump back into the seat, and seeing that car it reminds me of how I escaped.

But a chill came over me as I again continue to ask myself how have they found me?

Chapter 2

Lab Rat

Its 8am and as usual Mum is sitting at the side of my bed waiting for me to wake up. She has fresh cold orange juice and my daily tablets in hand.

"Morning sleepy head," she says as I open my eyes. Her warm loving smile is my most vivid memory. Someone I trusted, the person who I saw every day and told me never to be afraid. It was her that got me out, and I dread to think the price she had paid for it. Everyone she cared for called her Mum, but I was her only biological daughter. But no-one other than me and my dad knew that. This was her secret and if this was found out I don't know what they would of done to her.

8am on the dot I wake every day with no alarm clock needed, regardless of when I go to sleep, I just can't sleep past 8am. They say we all have a body clock but mine you can tell the time by it!

I sit up and smile rubbing my eyes to wake up. "Good morning," I say with a sleepy smile, yawning as I take the juice she is holding out for me. I gulp a couple of mouthfuls it tastes so refreshing, then she hands me the tablets three blue capsules, one round red pill and two white torpedos. I have to take them in order red, white and blue!

I grew up in the Sanctum, An old psychiatric institute in the middle of the Nevada Desert. A government facility with high security re-purposed for the Veritas Project. Now it's a government research facility specialising in genetic enhancements.

I was raised by two embryogenetic scientists Dr. Susan and Dr. Tom Edwards who were my parents. Susan was loving, kind and made me laugh. I remember she would always take the time to play games and read fairy tale princess stories to me every night where she would tell me, I was the princess. Tom on the other hand was distant and had no patience. He would get very agitated when I didn't do as I was told. Which when you are very young and a "little brat" as he called me can be very often. He was curt and exasperated with me in all our encounters. He was the parent that was the disciplinarian. When I misbehaved because I didn't want to do the tests anymore, he would lash out. As I got older, he became more aggressive. At the beginning he didn't know, but that's no excuse for his behaviour and I hate him!

Dr. Tom Edwards was a brilliant scientist, who looked more like a lawyer than a scientist. Under his white lab coat he was always in a smart sharp suit a Hugo Boss, Tom Ford or Brioni perhaps and always had to be a three piece and slim fitting. He had messy light-brown hair that gets lighter to the tips, always having to cut it short to keep it under control. Piercing green eyes that are dead, cold and with no emotion.

The first real memory of pain is when I was about eleven, "No daddy, I don't want to do this anymore, he smells. I don't like touching him." I remember as my mind drifts to a waking memory. He is walking towards me with that look that means this will hurt! He had no patience no control and never showed any remorse.

"Elly, don't start, just get on with it. We don't have time for your games today." He shouts as he puts his note book down on the nearby table and then grabs both my arms. With venom in his eyes he says shaking me with a raised voice, "Get on with it, if you don't you know what will happen." I just stare at him with pure defiance and he lets go of one of my arms and goes to his belt to start undoing it. I am thirteen years old now and for the last few years its been getting more and more aggressive. Should a thirteen year old know what it feels like to be hit by a leather belt, and all too regularly. I ask myself. "No Daddy," I say over and over. He lets go of me and I see his belt in his hand. He folds it double and lunges for me with his arm raised high holding the belt. A whoosh and he lands a blow, I scream in pain and curl into a ball. He carries on and after three more blows with ragged breath asks, "Enough?."

I look at him through streams of tears and nod. He runs his hands through his hair, adjusts his tie, and puts his belt back on. Composing himself by straightening his lab coat, he steps back picks up his notebook and gestures me to stand up.

I am shaking, and in excruciating pain from the beating he has just delivered, its more ferocious this time, but it's amazing what you get used to! Once I have steadied myself, I walk through the door into the lab area. At the same time, he leaves to go to the observation room.

Once through the door into the lab a man was sitting there, he was overweight, black hair, dark eyes and unshaven. He smells of alcohol and I can see tattoos under his shirt and all along his arms where he has ripped off both the sleeves. He must be about thirty, I think to myself. As I look up to the observation window, I hold out my hand to shake his hand. Suddenly the voice of Tom comes through to the lab. "Shake her hand," he commands. The man reaches forward, and we connect.

I blink rapidly for a few seconds and I know everything about the man who is shaking my hand. His whole life, his memories and I can also speak fluently his native tongue, Spanish. A dialect from a rural town in Mexico close to the Guatemala border called Los Margaritas.

Tom calls over the PA for me to say aloud the information I have just converted from this man. So, I begin. "Senior Emilio Esteban," I say.

I am interrupted suddenly by, "English Elly please," over the speakers. Because the last thought transferred is in a specific language I can either converse in that language or revert back to English, I usually show my defiance by remaining in another language other than English just to register my defiance.

"Emilio Esteban, aged thirty-six, from Los Margaritas, married to Manuela and has two children Julio and Alena." The man sitting there begins to sit upright and looks confused wondering what's going on and how do I know these things.

"Go on," comes sarcastically over the PA. "Just tell me what you want to know?" I say with steely defiance in my face. As I look directly into the camera in the corner of the room.

"Who does he work for?" I am asked.

"Santa Maria Cartel," I reply. The man begins to realise what's going on.

"No no," he says trying to say it's not true.

"Where is the next shipment going to take place?" A silent pause as I don't answer. He asks again in a more forceful tone.

I look over to Emilio and pause for a second then respond with, "leaving by private air strip 30km west from Los Margaritas."

"You're done for today," comes over the PA. As I leave the lab a guard comes in in military uniform, I can see his name badge briefly and only catch Joe. I continue and go back to my room. I run to my bed and curl up in ball. As I lay down, I feel sharp pain where he hit me and begin to cry.

My room is clinical - white with a large bed in the centre of the room. The left side of the room has a big window looking outside to the gardens with a door leading into the lab area, and on the right a large mirror almost the full width of the wall. The only thing making it less like a hospital room was the desk and cork board that I populated with pictures of animals trying to add something of me to this place. I am sure that my instincts always told me this was odd, and that my actions and behaviours to rebel were not just teenage angst but my subconscious telling me this is wrong.

I never knew anything different though, this was normal to me as I had nothing else to compare to. My parents or who I was told were my parents were scientists, the best in their field Embryogenetic. Basically, they played god with baby cells, removing bad ones and adding in new ones. Just to see what it did. I was patient 311Y and my mum hated that, so she called me Elly. But 311y was meant to be a boy as the Y chromosome is only male. But my cell division decided to be different and so here I am Elly x. From that moment I have been monitored for sixteen years under microscope, lab tested and studied without any interactions outside of the Institute staff.

My mum comes in and tells me how great I was as she soothes away the hair from my face. She wipes the tears away gently with her hand and opens her arms for me fall into. I clamber to her as I feel safe when she is there. As she puts her arms around me to comfort me, I wince.

She asks me, "What's wrong?" I just shake my head and can't look at her. She straightens me up and lifts my head with her hand under my chin. "It's ok sweetheart," Tell me what's wrong?" I know there is no use to avoid the answers as she will not let it drop. I sit up and raise my shirt, exposing my skin showing all the bruises from the lashes administered by my father earlier on in the day. My skin was red, purple and in places almost black.

I can't look her in the eye as I know it was my fault ." I hear her gasp in horror. "Oh My god," she says, "What happened? Who did this?"

"I was naughty," I said. "I didn't want to go into the lab." She pulls me in close that stops me talking anymore and holds me tight and I wince again.

"Sorry sweetheart." But I hear her under her breath, "Oh my god," saying it over and over again. She looks at me and smiles trying to make me feel better, but I can see she is upset. She is staring at the mirror in my room and shaking her head.

"You are going to be ok sweetheart, Let me get some medicine for you." She kisses my forehead and leaves by the main door. Pacing with a purpose!

She is in the hallway just outside my room and I hear raised voices. "Did you do that to Elly?" she is screaming at my dad and almost hysterical. She realised it was my dad and went to confront him. I run over to the door and put my ear against it to begin listening to them arguing. "How could you," she shouts.

"Susan calm down, you know how she gets," he tries to reason with her.

"Get your hands off me," she shouts at him. "She's your daughter. How could you, you heartless bastard"!

Then I hear footsteps moving away, its sound like clack clacks of stilettoes. My mum must have left. Then I hear more heavier footsteps and my dad must have gone after her.

I think that was the moment, that changed everything.

Before that point Tom was not aware, I was his biological daughter!

Chapter 3

Pamela

I am back in the now and realise I have tears streaming down my face. I wipe away the tears and compose myself as I need to find somewhere to stay tonight. The flashbacks happen without warning and I have no control over them. I look around to see if anyone has noticed me playing statues, luckily its dark and not many people are out on the streets. Every time a flashback happens, I am paralysed I can't move, speak or hear anything, I am back in that moment reliving the event. As I begin walking away from the bus stop, I head towards the beach, there is usually somewhere I can get a couple of hours sleep on a bench maybe or doorway. There are usually always toilets and showers near the beach so I can freshen up in the morning too. As I walk, I notice a nice quaint coffee shop, so I stop and make a note of the opening time, its 8am – perfect!

Luckily for me there are a few rough sleepers on the beach so I know its somewhere that I can rest and not be moved on by local cops. After a good twenty minutes walking up and down the beach, I see my spot! Barefoot Café on the beach. It has a large deck, and to one side is a fenced-off area where they must keep their bins and rubbish etc. But on the other side and to the front they have a large couple of sail's over the dining area, all the tables and chairs stacked nicely at the back protecting the bi-fold doors into the café. I can sleep under the tables that are stacked as me and my bags will fit, and it will shade me from any rain or wind.

Mind made up as this is the spot for the night, I walk towards the deck. A gentle voice tells me, "no don't go there." I look around and see a young guy about my age sleeping under a bench.

"Why not?" I ask.

"They come in early about 6am, if they find you, they call the cops."

"Oh, ok thanks," I reply. I start to walk away, and he calls back to me.

"You can share this bench with me if you want," he smiles. I am really not sure, so I thank him and start to move away, he insists "All the good spots are taken by this time." He adds, "have you just arrived?"

I realise it's so late and I am exhausted. "Yes, just got in," I say as I think to myself, I have nothing he can steal. He gestures me to take the bench itself and he will move to the floor. How kind I think, why would he do that.

"Your new here aren't you?" he asks.

I nod. I take my bags off and rest them on the bench and lie on top of them, leaving my LV still around my body. I am exhausted and need to rest. I lay on top of my bags and before I can blink, I am asleep.

I am woken by someone shaking me.

"Hey, wake up the cops are coming… girl wake up." My eyes start to open and its him the kind boy from last night. "We gotta go," he says he's all worked up and agitated. As I realise the drill, my senses wake up and I bolt upright. Rough sleepers are always moved on. It's almost an unwritten rule. Just be gone before a shop opens or joe public can see you.

I check to make sure I have everything, my LV is safe and put on my 2 rucksacks. "Hey," I shout to the boy, "Thanks for looking out for me."

"No worries, I'm Jessy by the way, see you around maybe?"

He moves off at speed. I adjust my bags for comfort and try to figure out the way back to that quaint coffee shop I saw yesterday. Everywhere is so different in the daylight, I look out at the ocean and wow- so beautiful. I just stand for a couple of minutes watching all the movements, ripples and shimmering colours. Cobalt blue, aquamarine and sapphire. Its early must be 6a.m. or thereabouts, and I can see swimmers already in the water for their daily swim. I smile as I wish that was me too. As I watch I hear a growling noise coming from my stomach.

Luckily, I find my way back to the café I spotted last night. Helpful that it's situated on the road directly between the bus stop and the beach. As I push open the Café door an old fashioned bell rings, everyone sitting the café looks towards me. I feel a little embarrassed, maybe as I have just got off a park bench after sixteen hours of travelling on a bus. I image I look like an Alice Cooper fan from all the crying that I have done in the last twenty four hours and I have all my worldly possessions in two rucksacks. So, I must also look like a hopeless hobo.

A smile and "Hi there" comes from the lady behind the counter. She must be in her late forties, blonde hair tied in a bun, a lot of make up on but you can see natural beauty behind all that. Beautiful deep-brown eyes that offer mystery and compassion. Friendly and welcoming just by her demeanour, a little overweight but you can see she has a happy disposition.

I smile and make eye contact. As I walk to the counter the smell of the food makes my stomach growl. The lady smiles and lets out a little giggle, "Hungry doll?"

I respond with, "Everything smells so good in here."

"Thanks doll, what can I get ya?"

"Erm, a regular flat white and just some sourdough toast please."

"Sure, doll do ya want jam and butter?" She asks.

I nod and smile. I pay cash and take a seat at the front in one of the big old fashion windows so I can start surveying the surroundings, keeping a watchful eye out.

After what seems like only a short while she is at the side of me with my order. "Thank you," I say as she puts the last piece of my order in front of me.

She puts a hand on my shoulder that somehow makes me feel safe and replies, "No worries doll, just shout if ya need anything else, my name is Pamela."

I smile and nod in understanding. "I'm Hannah, Hannah Roberts," I reply leaving the last name of Zoe Shaw behind me, new place means new identity.

This toast and Jam tastes so good, I can't remember when I last ate. As I think about it, it's usually me and Duke once we finish setting up in the café, we get 10 minutes before he opens the doors. Oh no Duke! My mind drifts back to yesterday and the recovery team from Veritas. I hope he is ok. I want to ring the hospital to see how he is, did he make it? Then I tell myself that I can't, I have to leave it all behind me now or they will trace me here. I hold back the tears and sniff and take my last sip of coffee.

As I stand Pamela is back to clear my table. "Thank you, that hit the spot," I said with a grateful smile.

"Glad to hear it," she replies. "See you again," she calls after me as I make my way out onto the street.

I raise my hand in acknowledgement and wave goodbye. I can sense she is a good person; I tell myself and aim to visits the coffee shop again.

Day one in a new place, mental checklist… nourishment – check and damn good that was too, I think to myself licking my lips. Home-made plum jam. Mmmmmnnn! So, first thing is first, let's find somewhere to stay. I head back towards the beach area to look for shops. I have always found private lettings through shop window adverts and this means less questions. I walk up and down looking in the windows for private advertisers of rooms to rent or something similar. I notice a faded advert for a room above a local shop. I scramble in my LV to find a pen and write the telephone number on the back of my hand. I go into the shop and ask the man behind the counter if he knows where there is a nearby payphone. He looks at me puzzled, I think to myself ok everyone has cell phones these days, so to change his thinking I say, "my cell has died but I need to ring my mum." He nods in that Oh I see kind of way and smiles. He tells me just keep walking another block outside the bakery there is a payphone. I thank him and head towards the bakery.

Its only 8am and I feel the temperature rising. I am hot and carrying my two bags which is like having a hot water bottle strapped to me. As I turn the corner of the block, I see the bakery and the payphone. Heading towards this I see Jessy running towards me. As he passes me, he smiles and says, "Hey girl," then in a flash he is gone followed by what look like two store security guards. They glance at me because he has spoken to me and I just shrug my shoulders as they look in my direction.

I reach the payphone and scramble for change out of my LV. Luckily, change from the toast this morning has provided the right coins to make this call. I dial the number I wrote on the back of my hand and a familiar voice answers the phone. "Erm," hearing this voice puts me off guard.

"Yes doll can I help you?"

"I have seen your advert for a room to let, is it still available?"

"Yes doll," comes back quickly.

"Please could I come and view?" I ask. "Sure, we are open till 6pm, It's the Coffee Shop on the Main Boulevard," she replies.

I realise its Pamela from the coffee shop I have just had breakfast in. Wow spooky coincidence I think to myself.

"Ok great thanks," I reply, "Is it ok to come over now?" I ask.

"Sure Doll, perfect time," she replies.

I hang up and head back as quickly as I can, I tell myself this is fate and it's a sign that its going to be a good thing.

I ask myself is my luck changing?

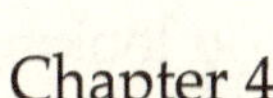

Chapter 4

New Apartment

Again, as I walk back into the coffee shop the bell chimes behind me from the door.

"Back again," says Pamela with a smile.

"Erm, I just rang you regarding the room you have," I responded in a shy and embarrassed tone.

"Yeah doll come this way," she says and shouts over to the kitchen area at the back "Loulou can you watch the front for me doll?"

A distance voice replies with a, "sure, I'll be right there."

Pamela gestures me to come through to the kitchen area, it's a tight squeeze with all my bags on, but I am careful not to be a clutz! As we head out of the kitchen there is a steel spiral staircase leading to a big wooden door. We head up the stairs and she unlock the door.

Its amazing! When I look inside a studio flat with polished wooden floors, the biggest bed I have ever seen at the back on the raised level and just the right amount of space for cooking for one! The sofa looks new or hardly used and all the furnishing seem to be really smart, plush and looks so comfy. Without thinking I blurt out, "Wow this is amazing."

She lets out a laugh, "Aw thanks doll it not much but I have good memories here." I try not to look to eager, but this would be like the fairy tale stories read to me every night by my mum if I lived here.

 "Erm, how much are you looking for?" I ask.

She looks me up and down and smiles, "can you afford $300 a month?" She asks.

I can't believe it, its beautiful, cheap… what's the catch? I ask myself.

"Well?" she asks,

"Yes, I'll take it, if you'll have me?" I reply smiling as sweetly as I can.

"I don't have any references am afraid, but I am clean and tidy, and I am very good as a tenant and I don't smoke or drink and…"

She holds up her hand for me to stop. She just smiles.

"This place is a palace and I will look after it I…"

she holds her hand up again to stop me for the second time. "Yes, it's yours doll," she says. "Can you afford the rent in advance?"

I nod and turn away to discreetly find the money in my LV.

Once we have exchanged the money, she hands me the key.I ask her, "why is it so cheap?"

She looks at me, pauses and says, "we all need a helping hand from time to time doll, and you look like you could do with one."

I bite my lip as to hold back the tears that are welling up, she has showed me so much kindness and I have only known this amazing person for a couple of hours. Again, she puts her hand on my shoulder and says, "I'll let you get settled doll." Turns and closes the door behind her.

This is amazing, I drop my bags where I stand feeling so amazed at this place as I start to look around, I just know that this is a sign of good things.

So, after composing myself and realising I have just landed the most amazing apartment, that also offers some protection as it is nicely out of the way and not easy to find, I begin to unpack. With such a frantic exit from Helen Town and just gathering everything I could, stuffing it into my bags I have clean and dirty washing all together.

I take a look around the apartment, opening doors and cupboards to see whether there is anything in them. I open the door to the bathroom and find a washing machine and dryer in there. "Fantastic," I say aloud. I open the cupboard under the sink just to see if my luck is holding, and look to see if there is any washing detergent in there. Eureka! There is. I rush back into the main room and gather up the pile of washing I had dumped on the floor that needs washing.

I do the usual dance with the washing machine trying to figure out which button to press and how to select the wash cycle. Luckily this is a front-loading machine and it has an on button, a dial and that's it. So, I select the program and once I've added the detergent I press on! I wait to hear that thud as the water suddenly begins to rush through the pipes before I continue to explore.

The kitchen which is part of the main living area has everything I need; kettle, toaster, microwave, all crockery, cutlery and glassware. I just can't believe my luck, and I realise that I haven't stopped grinning like a cheshire cat since I had the key put in my hand. For the first time in as long as I can remember this feels like a sanctuary. A place of solace and retreat that is just for me. No tests, no pain, just freedom.

Now that everything has been unpacked, well it took all of five minutes based on the limited number of things I own. But I don't care about possessions except maybe one thing. I have a silver locket with a picture of my parents inside and its my only treasure that I have that tells me I wasn't just a lab rat or experiment. If it wasn't for her, I don't know what would have happened to me.

I hold it in my hand and smile a sad smile as I know I will never see her again if she is still alive. The last thing she said to me was, "Don't look back monkey, keep running and never reveal to anyone what you can do. Trust no-one." Then she was gone.

I bring myself back to the now and push all the sadness out of my mind.

Chapter 5

Violent Memories

So, Elly what is the plan, what are you going to do now? I ask myself. I think I need a shower. After the travelling and sleeping on the beach a freshen up is definitely what's needed. I search out some clean clothes that I can get away with not ironing. Jeans and a white sleeveless linen shirt simple but smart/casual and put them on the bed. I had noticed some towels hanging in the bathroom, so I check them and give them a good sniff to see if they are clean. They smell lovely and fresh as though they have just been washed.

Grabbing my toiletries from my bag I head into the bathroom. I turn on the shower and begin to undress, I check the water with my hand. As is starts to get warm I step in and let it rush over me.

It feels so good to be clean and fresh. Taking one of the towels I have found, I wrap it around my hair and then another one around my body. Wiping away the steam on the mirror with my hand I look at myself and it triggers a flashback… I drift into a nightmare.

"Elly open the door," he shouts as his fist is thumping on the door. "I won't tell you again Elly open it now!"

"Go away," I screech back, sobbing into my hands. Scrunched up in the farthest corner of the room. I hear a commotion outside and a number of footsteps.

"You – Get something to break this god damn door down," I hear him shout. "NOW." He continues to bang on the door. As there is all sorts of noise and commotion outside the door, I hear stilettoes, I think it's Susan my mum.

"What's going on Tom?" she asks in a frantic voice. Thank goodness she is here he won't hurt me if she is here, I tell myself.

"Elly is having one of her tantrums again," he replies. "She has locked herself in the bathroom," he continues "You know who is arriving today," he say in a more hushed tone.

"Elly darling, are you ok? Come out its ok," she says through the door.

Then more noise and I guess who ever went to get something to break the door down, I expect one of the orderlies, Joe probably as he is always on my wing, comes back.

"Ok," I shout back, and it goes all quiet. "But if I see anyone else, I am coming straight back in here," I say my voice matching my body shakily and without conviction as I am holding back the tears. "Yes, ok sweetheart, but I need to make sure you are ok first," Mum shouts back in her kind and soft tone.

I clamber to my feet holding on to the basin cabinet to steady me. I wipe the tears and rub the back of my hand over my nose where it has been running. Slowly I reach the door and it clicks as I unlock it.

As I open the door Tom lunges forward to grab me and I scream.

"STOP," Susan shout and holds out her hand to block Tom coming forward. "Everyone out," she says, "Including you" as she turns to Tom.

"But," he starts to reply, and she holds up her hand to cut him off and begins pointing to the door. Her steely determination is not to be trifled with!

Once everyone has gone, she turns to me smiles and says, "C'mon Monkey its ok come out, what's going on?"

What do I say? "I don't feel well," I said. "I don't want to do the tests today… why do I have to?" I ask.

"Sweetheart, you know why!" "And you know that you are a very special part of that," she explains watching every expressions that I make. "You have made such a difference; and it's because you are so special," she tells me with a loving smile. "Plus, we have a special visitor today who is really important." She explains trying to be upbeat, she pauses waiting for me to answer. "Ok," she says after a short while looking me from side to side and tilting her head to one side, "No tests today, go have a shower and freshen up and I will come back in a little while to check on you and see if you feel any better," she says. "Have you eaten?" I shake my head. "Ok, I will bring you some soup." I smile as I like soup and it means she will be back again soon.

I go back into the bathroom and start the shower, holding my hand under the water to feel the temperature. It is warming up, so I get undressed and get in. The soothing water feels good, I just stand under the warm water letting it just rush all over me. A time goes by and I wash my hair and turn off the shower. Wrapping a towel around my hair and one around my body I stand in front of the mirror. Wiping away the steam with my hand I look at myself and see handprints on my arms, bruises on my shoulders, I loosen the towel and look at my ribs they are black and purple. He was really angry this time. I was only fourteen years old this time, and a couple of days from turning fifteen.

As I blink, I realise it's just a memory. Looking into the mirror I can see no bruises and I feel no pain. But a tear rolls down my face. How can anyone who claims they love you inflict so much pain on someone?

That was the last time before I escaped!

Chapter 6

Jessy

The last stroke of mascara on my eyelashes is done and I look into the mirror, yes that will do. Not too much makeup but a little window dressing has never hurt anyone, my mum would say.

I think of my mum and just how beautiful she was, beautiful blue eyes that shine like sapphires, they are so warm and Loving expressing very feeling she has. She has beautiful long dark-brown hair that shimmers with coppers and reds, she always looks immaculate! She has a habit of tucking one side of hair behind her ear showing off beautiful diamond drop earrings. She always wore make up, but her complexion was flawless. She was stunningly beautiful with a beautiful heart too. I miss her so much.

I pick up my LV and head out of the door. Let's explore!

So, first things first, now I feel refreshed, clean and ready for anything, usual drill new identity needs papers. If they find me where do I go? it's all about strategy and the preparation for a quick escape.

At the bottom of the spiral staircase I can see an alley way, this must lead to the main street alongside the café. I walk through to the main street. Instead of heading towards the beach this time I go in the opposite direction towards the bus stop.

Handy, I thought as I look at my watch, exactly three minutes' walk. I look at the times for departures. Damn only two per day, 6am and 2pm. This makes it difficult if I need to go in a hurry. But looking closer I can see that there are a number of pass through services every fifteen minutes during the day, where it picks up or drops off between nearby towns. The nearest main hub for me is Berrington which is roughly about twenty kilometres from here. Which is the two departures time for connections across the country.

I look around to see if there is any other transport here maybe a a train station. Nope! and I tut at myself as in my haste I may have restricted my chances of a getaway, if I need another out there isn't one. I make a mental note to myself that I need to explore the journey to Berrington, so I have my full strategy in place and get in my mind the lay of the land, the travel time etc. So, I am ready.

As I turn around and go to take a step, I notice across the way that I am being stared at, watched even. As I manage to focus my eyes through the sun, I see its Jessy. He seems to be a little taller than me, dark hair, blue eyes and square jaw. The rugged type, symmetrical face that makes him very handsome. He has an amazing smile that lights up his face, but he also has a shyness that makes him very likeable. He smiles and waves.

"Hey Girl," he shouts. I respond with a wave. He has an all-over golden tan wearing khaki cargo shorts and his white t-shirt flung over his shoulder. I walk over to him and just as I go to speak, he says, "leaving already?"

I smile and shrug off his comment. "No just checking it out, in case of emergencies," I say. "Are you stalking me?" I ask.

Jessy lets out a loud laugh and shakes his head. "No of course not, stalker that's a new one. I haven't been called that before," he says with the most captivating smile I have ever seen.

I feel myself blushing. I don't know how to respond or where to look. I am not used to talking to anyone really outside of the Sanctum staff and then it was pretty much only the orderlies and my parents.

"So, what are you up to?" he asks. "Do you wanna grab a drink or something?"

I don't know why but I want to say yes for some reason, but I know I can't I need to focus on the plan just in case I tell myself, "Erm, I can't at the minute sorry," I say, and I am really hoping he will ask me again.

He smiles and steps towards me, "So what are you doing that means you can't spend any time with me?" He asks.

I step back as I am not sure what's he's going to do. "I have only just arrived and need to get my bearings in this new place," I reply shakily with a tentative smile. I look around to see if anyone else is around as he is quite forthright in his charming british accent, but I am not sure what he wants.

"Really?" he adds with a mischievous smile, he has his arm folded with one hand resting under his chin taping one finger on his cheek. "I can show you around if you like?" He says and tilts his head to one side trying to look me in the eye. "You have the most beautiful eyes," he says, "I have never seen any so green." I don't know what to say I feel my cheeks warm and I blush again, is he doing it on purpose? I think to myself, but I just smile and look to the floor, my inner voice is challenging me to let him. My fear of being caught is a different matter. It's like I have two voices one on each shoulder whispering into my ear.

"Maybe some other time," I say as I start to move away.

I think he senses that I am not sure about him and he looks quite concerned with his brow all creased and that amazing smile is no longer evident anymore. He holds one of his hands up saying gently, "Hey its ok, no problem sorry if I seem a little pushy I don't mean to be. I like you and thought we could just hang out and get to know each other, after all I did share my bed with you last night!" His voice is quieter and more apologetic, and the smile is appearing again on his beautiful face. I stop and look at him and remember the kindness he offered when I first arrived.

So, after a small pause I say, "Ok I'm sorry, yes please I have a couple of hours spare that would be great if you could show me around," looking up at him, giving me an out if I need it by giving him a time frame.

"I'm Hannah by the way," I add.

He puts his hands on his hips and says, "Well alright then Hannah I will take what I can get let's go." Out stretching his arm gesturing me to walk forward we begin to walk away from the bus stop. Maybe this is a good thing I tell myself; I can get a lay of the land quicker by someone more familiar.

Jessy never shuts up. He has so much to say and I find myself just smiling like a lovesick schoolgirl and with the occasional nod of my head so that he knows I am still listening. By the time we walk into the main town, I know all about his sisters, three of them Julie, Diane and Charlotte. His parents with his Uncle Joseph running the family business in London, all about cargo and planes he tells me. He went to private schools and graduated with first class honours in Law. He calls his friends chums, that I find so funny. He stops for a moment and says, "Your turn, I have been talking for hours."

I just smile and say, "I like listening to you, you have great stories to tell.Please tell me more," I plead.

He smiles looks around and says, "Are you hungry? let's get something to eat, I know a place."

"Ok," I say, and he grabs my hand and starts to walk. I instantly shake my hand out of his and stop. I see a flash of his memory his sisters, parents and Uncle Joseph. He looks at me puzzled. "Jessy, I don't know you, I'm sorry I think I need to go." Before he can respond I am at a pace heading off in the opposite direction to him heading back to my place.

I hear him behind me shouting, "Hey Hannah what's wrong? C'mon don't be like that." His voice is fading as I quicken the pace.

I arrive back at the alley by the café. I hear footsteps behind me. I turn to look and "Jessy," I say alarmed and surprised.

"Look," he says panting from the brief jog he has just done to catch up with me. "I'm sorry if I overstepped the mark, sincerely I am. We seem to be hitting it off and I just wanted to, well I was just being friendly," he says. "I really didn't mean to upset you," he continues. "Please don't be mad at me you are the first person I have met in a long time that I want to spend some time with, you are cool girl," he says with that smile exploding all over his face.

I can't help it I sense he is being genuine, and I feel the smile appear on my face. "You're forgiven," I say.

"Yes," he exclaims with a fist pump. "So, shall we eat?" he asks. Feeling quite hungry at this point and as we have reached the café, I can smell the baking that makes my mouth water.

"Sure," I say with a smile and walk towards him. "This place is great for food and Pamela the lady owner seems lovely," I tell him.

"This was where I wanted to take you," he says. "The homemade Jam here is to die for," he says licking his lips. I look at him and I think to myself wow I had the jam this morning and it was delicious.

We go into the café with the door chiming as usual and I wave and smile at Pamela who gives a great big welcoming smile back. She winks at me as she sees Jessy appear from behind me and we take a seat in the window.

"What can I get ya," Pamela says as she arrives at our table. Jessy gestures to me to go first.

"Do you have any scones," I ask?

"Sure, do doll, just outta the oven, you want cream and jam?" She asks.

"Oh yes please," I add.

"Any drinks doll?," Pamela adds.

"Oh yes, Earl Grey please," I reply.

Jessy jumps in, "I'll have the same please." "How very British of you," he says.

I frown, "What do you mean?" I ask.

"A cream tea," he explains.

Pamela leaves and starts to get our order ready. I must look puzzled as he explains to me what afternoon tea consists of. But his statement is kind of weak now he had to explain the reference. I make light of it by telling Jessy I have never visited England.

I have always drunk tea in particular Earl Grey, so did my mum. We would enjoy afternoons in my room with a tray that has a teapot filled with Earl Grey tea leaves and it had to be leaves she would tell me, plus only china cups and saucers. With a selection of the essential assorted biscuits to dunk in the tea!

As our order arrives at the table, the teapot with cups and saucers triggers my mind. As it drifts back, Mum walks in my room with her tray. A beautiful white bone china teapot with a single gold ring for design. two cups and saucers, and a small plate containing digestives biscuits. "So, Elly how's today been?" she asks.

"Good," I say but without any eye contact.

"Elly, what's wrong darling?" she adds.

I look up and smile, "Why *am* I doing this?"

She straightens the hair across my forehead and says, "The information you provide helps us to fight against bad people. stop them from killing, stop them selling drugs and makes safe this world. You see the truth," she exclaims, "That is so important. None of the others have anywhere near your abilities," she says.

"What others?" I ask quizzically. She looks at me shocked and then a frightened thought seems to appear in her mind scared as though she should not have told me that. "Mum, what others?" I ask again.

"Elly, please don't ask me that," she says. "I should not have said anything." She continues, "For your safety forget I said that PLEASE," she pleads. "Tell me you understand?" she says and grabs my hands. She looks at me and a tear falls down her cheek.

I am scared for a moment, as there is desperation in her voice. She lets go of one of my hands and wipes away the tear, she kisses my forehead.

"OK' I say.

Normally with a touch I can read every thought a person has ever had, change their memory too if I need to. But not with my mum, she and my dad are the only ones I can't read. Blood relative! I was around ten years old the headache had gone, and it was the first time I had managed to open my eyes for what felt like weeks, but it was only two days. I felt different but wasn't sure how. In the next lab session, I would find out.

Every time my abilities evolve it starts with a debilitating headache. At first it was just seeing images from people I have been in contact with when I was about five years old. At that age I could not understand what it was, it just scared me and I refused any contact as I was not able to process the thoughts transferring to me. Then after the next headache I was able to control my ability and actually search in the mind of another, delve through their past and be able to communicate in any language even dialects of remote areas. What transferred to me was their native tongue as if I grew up with them. Even at ten-years old this is still quite frightening, but I never felt scared of what I was doing as my mum this amazing woman always reassured me it was ok, I was safe, and no one could hurt me. It seems every five years a headache would come and add to my abilities and as predicted at fifteen the biggest headache happened this lasted for five days. Now I can project memories and erase ones that previously existed. My orders were to remove any knowledge of the institute to everyone I had contact with.

I am now nineteen and my birthday is in two months' time, so I expect another headache as it always comes as a birthday gift!

"Hannah… earth to Hannah planet… hey Hannah where are you?," Jessy is trying to get my attention. I blink and the flashback has gone. "Hey dreamer girl," he says. "Where did you drift off too?"

"Just thinking of my mum," I said. "Sorry." and changing the subject quickly I say, "Oh these smell delicious," as Pamela has delivered the food to our table.

We enjoy the afternoon tea as Jessy called it and I urge him to continue telling me his stories, it's fascinating and I can't stop watching his face. How he smiles when he talks about his sisters. Our eyes are locked in a deep gaze and I can sense all of his emotions with every word he says. I just rest my temple against my fist, my elbow on the table and lean towards him listening.

He looks at me and laughs.

"What's so funny?" I say as I sit up.

"Am I boring you?" he asks. "You look like you are falling asleep."

"No," I giggle. "I love your stories; they are so great," I add. "I don't have brothers or sisters, so I don't know what that is like," I point out.

"So, you're an only child," Jessy points out. "That explains it," he says.

"Explains what?" I ask. "Why you wouldn't let me hold your hand," he replies.

"Oh yes," I say sheepishly. I feel embarrassed and I know I am blushing as that warm sensation is filling my face.

"It's ok," he says. "I get it."

There is one scone left on the plate and I look at Jessy and have a wicked grin, "Dibs on the scone," I say changing the subject. I quickly grab the scone and put it on my plate.

Jessy laughs, "It's been a long time since I've heard that expression," he says. "My chums at St. Lancelot used to say it all the time" he adds.

"Was that your school name?" I ask. He nods. As I cut open the scone and fill one piece of it with cream and jam, I offer this half to Jessy. He looks surprised but nods and opens his mouth. I stuff the scone in and laugh. He takes hold of a bit of scone that is sticking out of his mouth and just shakes his head at me, as he chews the mouthful and smiles at the same time. I add the last bit of cream and jam to the remaining piece of scone and begin to eat. The last sip of tea washes down the scone and I sigh a deep sigh of contentment.

"What would you like to do now?" Jessy asks me with that amazing smile all over his face.

"let's go to the beach," I say, I want to spend time with him and be in his company. Forgetting all my plans that is not like me at all and just wanting the time with Jessy.

"Yeah good idea," Jessy says. We stand together and head over to the counter to pay for our food. Jessy turns to me and says, "A gentlemen pays," and hands over his credit card to Pamela.

"No," I protest, "let me pay for mine at least," I insist.

"No, I insist," he says determined.

Pamela Looks at us both and as she looks Jessy up and down, she shakes her head with a mischievous smile and says, "Hmmm gentleman, not many of them about doll." I say my thanks so does Jessy and we leave the café to head to the beach.

As we arrive at the beach, I can't wait to slip off my sandals and feel the sand under my feet, "I love the sea," I say without any prompt.

"Me too," says Jessy, in a tone that he seems to be surprised by my unsolicited statement.

We find a spot on the sand and sit just staring out at the shimmering water. A few boats are visible in the distance with sails billowing in the gentle breeze, the sun low as it's early evening. Turning his head towards me Jessy asks, "Are you going to tell me anything about you?"

"There's not much to tell," I reply staring out to the horizon.

"So, where are you from as you are not an Aussie,," he asks. "I can't quite figure out your accent?" He leans back on both his elbows that become buried into the sand. "I've been spilling my guts on everything about me, I'm an open book," he adds. "I only want to get to know you," he says with a gentle reassuring tone.

I think to myself that I have to offer some explanation but not enough to warrant more questions, so I begin to explain my story, which is not usual for me. Everywhere that I have been up to now never required any explanation or chit chat.

I think as long as it's a reasonably truthful story leaving out the weird stuff, I think to myself it will be ok. My inner voice is saying "Why I am trying to convince myself to make this conversation?" I can't quite put my finger on it. So, I begin cautiously looking at my fingers or out to the sea doing everything I can not to have eye contact.

"I grew up in the US," I reply. "But I have been in Australia now for a couple of years," I add trying to remain vague. "I left the US and travelled to Hawaii, then Fiji and then here I am Australia!... So how did you end up in Australia?" I ask Jessy changing the focus back to him.

"Oh that's a long story," he says, "Another time. I have done my talking for today it's you I want to get to know," he continues "I want to know more about you Hannah." His voice changes to a soft silky tone that make me feel warm and excited at the same time. He is intoxicating.

I find keeping to the truth as much as possible has always been the best strategy, leaving out the weird abilities part and being hunted by clever but ruthless government mercenaries. The real grey areas are the actual detail of who I am and where I came from. "So, what do you want to know?" I ask Jessy feeling confident that I can give him a story that will suffice to close the subject.

"Tell me about your parents, schools you attended, friends everything," he adds as he lays down resting his head on his interlocked fingers behind his head.

"Wow life story huh," I exclaim. He turns his head and just smiles as he nods. Cautiously I begin, "Erm my parents are scientist…"

"What kind?" he says interrupting my flow.

"No idea," I reply looking at my hands. I hate lying and I know I am terrible at it.

"They work in a lab and wear a white coat, all that science stuff," I add trying to seem bored. "Boring!" I exclaim.

That makes Jessy laugh. "Go on," he says.

"Well I am an only child, so no idea what it's like to have brothers and sisters, and I was home schooled."

Jessy sits up and responds quickly with astonishment, "Really, home schooled?"

"Yes," I say looking quizzical at him. "Why is that strange to you?" I question him.

"Well it's not strange," he says "But it is a little weird," he says shrugging his shoulders. I don't know what to say to that. I am not sure if I am upset or angry. I look at him and just when I was about to speak, Jessy says, "I'm sorry, I don't mean to be rude. My brain to mouth filter does not always work when it should. so… you are an only child, you were home schooled, and I guess don't have any school friends, so who were your friends when you were growing up?" he asks, as he is more interested in everything I say now. I seem to have fuelled his fire for being nosey!

I am not sure what to say, as his response has thrown me off guard making me slightly annoyed. I think he can see my reluctance. I can't say Oscar the orderly! He is going to think I am really weird. I can't really explain that the only person outside of the Sanctum staff such as my parents, orderlies and occasional military personnel who I spoke to were criminals. What can I say I ask my inner self?

"Erm I found it difficult to make friends when I was younger as we moved around a lot, hence the home school so I didn't really have many friends," I add by way of an explanation. Hoping this will suffice! Jessy looks at me and seems to be ok with my response. He says nothing waiting for me to carry on.

I continue with, "It's not all bad though, if you don't know any better you can't miss anything," I say with a fake smile and shrug of my shoulder.

Jessy just looks at me and smiles, "Its ok" he says. "I don't judge you. I am just trying to get to know you. I like you Hannah, you're different," he says, "and I really like that." I lay on my side with my head resting across my folded arm and Jessy mirrors me.

"Your turn," I say cheekily biting my lip hoping he will oblige, "How long have you been in Terra Hope?" I feel very pleased with myself in changing the subject back to him.

"About six months on and off." He continues, "I decided to go travelling, so here I am." I left London and came to Australia. First Melbourne then Sydney and then began travelling the coast, and here I a.m. ," he exclaims. "what made you come here?" he asks.

"Same," I say playfully, and we both laugh. "I love the sea and find inner peace from the ocean."

"Oh, you're not going to start chanting are you?" Jessy says in a sarcastic tone.

"No," I laugh and flick sand at him. He opens his mouth in an O shape as he was surprised by my playfulness and flicked sand back at me. I giggle and sit up biting my bottom lip brushing more sand into Jessy's shirt.

He laughs and sarcastically replies "Really?" then rapidly starts brushing sand all over me.

I can't stop laughing, in between blowing out sand that is going into my mouth. Before I know it, I am cocooned in the sand and my hands are buried. Jessy looks at me and I am not sure what he is doing. He smiles and moves the hair out of my face tracing his finger over my cheek and down to my chin. He leans over and our lips touch as Jessy kisses me.

Chapter 7

Kissing

I must look horrified; Jessy looks at me for a reaction to his kiss and I am filled with panic. I start to wriggle out of the sand and stand up.

Jessy rises to his feet, "I'm sorry," he pleads. "I keep apologizing to you, I thought I could read you but I am getting it wrong every time," he pleads as he shakes his head and looks at his feet. I don't know why but I want to ease his turmoil.

Embarrassed I say "It's ok," quietly under my breath, "I have never been kissed before," I add innocently. "It's just a surprise."

He stops looks up at me and says in shock, "You've never been kissed before? really?." I nod. "Have you been locked in a tower, with a dragon guarding you?," he says cheekily. "How is that possible? you are the most mesmerising, beautiful creature I have ever seen," he claims.

I feel something towards Jessy but not really sure what it is, I start to feel the warmth in my cheeks as I know I blushing

47

but have never experienced this kind of feelings before for another person. I know we have connected in a way that's different to the gifted connections, I like it! I want to ease his confusion as he's not sure what is wrong, I can see his expressions asking himself is it him? is it me? and I am sure he has never met anyone, anything like me before. So, I offer an explanation by way of easing the tension.

"As I said before we travelled a lot, I never really hung out with anyone and my parents were pretty strict," I add. "Remember I'm not very good at making friends, I don't really know how to do it and well there has never been anyone that I wanted to kiss me…… until now," I explain smiling at Jessy waiting for him to catch up. Jessy smiles at me and pauses whilst he just stares at me, I can see his whole body relax as his shoulders drop, he seems much more comfortable now with the explanation.

"You are so special," he says in a hushed silky tone. He tilts his head over to one side and asks, "Did you like being kissed?"

I look at him and smile and feel my cheeks warm. "I'm not sure you can call that a kiss," I say cheekily.

His eyes open wide in amazement and moves towards me, his hands gently cup my face and he lean in. He pauses to get my acceptance. I don't move away, and he gently clasps his lips over my bottom lip. It sends a sweet sensation through my body that makes my mouth open. He takes full advantage and as he covers both my lips with his I feel his tongue, gently move into my mouth searching for mine. As if by freewill my tongue moves to meet his and as our tongues meet, and lips gently move over each other we are locked into an embrace that feels electrified.

We break apart and both with ragged breath looking into each other's eyes, I realise that my mind is blank. We have touched and I did not make a mind connection to read his thoughts. How is that possible I ask myself? the only other time is with mum and dad.

Jessy smiles at me and says, "Wow! you know how to kiss girl"! I smile at him and feel amazing without fear, and calm as my breathing returns to normal.

"Not so bad yourself," I say in a nonchalant way, having no idea what I am talking about and no reference to compare to.

He laughs and says, "C'mon let's get outta here."

"Where to?" I ask.

"My place," he says as a matter of fact. I look puzzled as he was sleeping on a bench about ten metres from where we were on the sand. He starts to move off the beach and ushers me to come along.

We head out past the café towards the bus stop and keep walking for about ten minutes. We walk along the road with nothing but open countryside all around us. Jessy stops suddenly and starts to climb over a fence, holding out his hand to help me. I ignore his hand and climb over with ease. Much to his surprise he struggled a little coming after me, his five foot ten inch height making the climb awkward. I see a tent in the distance.

"Is that yours?" I ask pointing to the tent.

"Si mi casa tu casa," he says.

"Gracias mi amigo," I reply.

"Hablas espanol?" He asks.

"Si por supesto," I add.

"So not just a pretty face then," he scoffs. "You speak fluent Spanish?"

"Yes," I reply not wishing to add any further details.

We arrive at his tent and he unzips the front, holds the flap open and nods his head in the direction of the entrance to gesture me to go in.

"This is nice," I say looking around. "So why the beach yesterday?" I ask.

"I just arrived back as the day was ending and didn't want to attempt putting the tent up in the dark so made the best of what I could find." He adds, " I do love it here and always seem to keep coming back no matter where I travel to." His explanation makes me curious for more.

So, I ask, "What do you mean by you keep coming back?" Looking at him for clarity and explanation.

"I have travelled around this area out to Berrington, as an example and spent a couple of weeks there but I don't know really, Terra Hope is just somewhere I feel at home." He sounds so content in the answer that makes me sigh as I wish I felt that.

As I look around his tent its quite roomy, a double air bed, a chair a lamp and cooking equipment. He has a number of books on the floor at the side of his air bed. They catch my eye. "What are you reading?" I ask.

"I like the classics," he replies. "Hans Christen Anderson at the moment, it's a collection of his stories."

"I love the little match girl," I interject. He looks at me surprised. "That's one of my favourites," he adds smiling. "I remember it from being a small boy and one of the stories my parents would read to me." His recollection makes him smile in a familiar way as I know I am doing the same recalling the stories my mum would read each night. He sits on his air bed and pats the bed for me to join him, I shake my head and sit on the chair opposite him.

I think he has begun to understand my shyness as he realises, I am cautious in my experiences with people and in particular the opposite sex. But I can't stop thinking about that kiss. Without realising it I am touching my lip with my thumb and index finger running along the outline of my lips, reliving the sensation.

"That good eh," Jessy laughs and I realise he has been watching what I have been doing.

I begin to stutter, embarrassed by being caught in my reverie. "I – I – I..."

"Its ok, am only teasing you," he says. "I really enjoyed it too. I want to do it again," he adds and looks steely at me to see how I react. I squirm in my seat, looking at my feet. Of course, I do, I shout in my head.

"Maybe," I add beginning to raise my head just enough to see his reaction.

He laughs out loud. "Well it's not a no," he says.

Jessy looks at his books and to ease the tension of the conversation he starts to talk about some of his favourite stories. We start to talk more about books we have read and share some of the stories. So many we have in common and for the first time in forever, I feel relaxed. We laugh about him reading what he called chick books - love stories, we both read chasing Harry Winston. We started talking about Dan Brown and he asked what I thought about the films, such as Da Vinci Code. How do I explain I have never watched a TV or seen a movie I can't really tell him that? I try to be evasive and he ask me, "What about the scene with the pope, skydiving to save the girl?"

I say, "yeah I guess a great scene," looking at my hands. He startles me as he moves very quickly and is kneeling in front of me.

He lifts my head with his hand under my chin, looks me in the eyes with a kind smile and say, "You haven't seen it have you?" I shake my head and look at him with tears pooling in my eyes.

All I can think is he is going to find out who I am, think I am weird and want nothing to do with me! I am scared and feel panic rising. Should I run I think to myself.

"Hey beautiful," he says calmly. "Its ok, I didn't mean to upset you." He continues, "Its ok if you haven't seen it, am only teasing." He strokes my cheek with his thumb, and I close my eyes enjoying his touch. A tear falls down my cheek and he rubs it away. "It's ok," he says reassuringly, and I feel the electricity as he gently kisses my cheek, my forehead, my other cheek and as I open my eyes, he kisses my lips.

He stops and looks at me and I smile I guess it's more of an acknowledgement telling him its ok. He stands up and holds out his hand for me to take it. I stand but don't take his hand. He steps closer and cups my face but both hands feel familiar and I close my eyes enjoying the sensation and we kiss with our tongues twisting together, our bodies pushing against each other. His hands begin to leave my face and he rests on my shoulders for a second before moving down my arms. He takes hold of my hands and I open my eyes; I hear his thoughts he is telling himself don't blow it, she is beautiful, clever, funny. He lets go of one hand and begins to walk backwards towards his air bed pulling me towards him.

I am captivated by him, electrified by him, almost in a trance and I can't resist, I don't want to resist. He lets go of my hand and I regain my composure, as though the connection has been broken.

"Are you ok?" Jessy asks.

"Yes," I reply. His hands are at my waist. He is unbuttoning my jeans. I grab his hands instinctively, "Stop"! I cry out. "I'm not ready," I say in panic.

Jessy stops straight away, and a look of panic has reached his face. "I'm sorry," he exclaims. "I thought you wanted me too." I hold my hand to his mouth to stop him.

"I'm sorry I have never done this before and it scares me a little, I am not sure I am ready," I say by way of explanation.

Jessy smiles. "It's ok, I am not going to rush you, I like you," he says with that amazing smile appearing across his face.

I am now feeling really embarrassed. I turn facing away from him looking at the way out, Jessy wraps his arms around me from behind and rests his chin on my shoulder. "You're so beautiful," he says as he pulls me into him. "I'm not going to rush you, I just want to spend time with you," he whispers into my ear.

He feels so warm and safe, I like being in his arms, resting my head against his. After a moment though it's time to leave as it feels a little awkward and I don't know what to do or say in that moment.

"Erm I think I should be getting back now. It's been quite a day all in all," I say without having to look at him as he still has his arms wrapped around me. He releases me and I turn to face him and say again, "Wow what a day"! trying to remove the awkwardness I feel he smiles at me and I think he is letting me know its ok. "I am glad I have met you Jessy," I tell him. As I move to leave, I continue to say, "Its ok I know my way back. "Stay." And I turn to leave.

"Hold on Hannah," he says. "Let me come with you it's dark and I was raised to be a gentleman," he exclaims with a very posh British accent. "You can stay here you know, it's more comfortable than the beach." I roll my eyes as I know I can take care of myself, but I do like his company, then I realise he thinks I am still sleeping rough. So, I nod with acceptance that he can walk me back.

We head out over the fence back to the main road. An eerie silence between us in the total darkness, my inner voice is shouting at me to say something.

"So, the other day when you ran past me," I say, "you were being chased, what was that all about?"

Jessy stumbles in his response. "Err nothing really. It was a misunderstanding," he points out matter of fact.

"Really?" I reply very sarcastically.

He sighs. "I, well you see," he sounds so uncomfortable surely, it can't be that bad.

"It's ok," I say stopping him, "you don't owe me an explanation, I am just making conversation," I explain. "It's a dark lonely road so just making sure you are still there," I say. Next thing I feel him grab my hand.

"Now you know I am here," he replies.

I hold tight of his hand as the connection to his memories are made. I see his school, friends, his sisters and the mischief he played on his friends. Birthday parties, graduations, university, everything in a second of his life to that point. His last memory I can see is his argument with his father over his allowance and that unless he joins the family business there would be no more allowance. His mum however defies his father and sends him money every month. As we near to my apartment I say, "This is me," pointing to the Alley way next to the café. He lets go of my hand and I blink to clear my mind.

"Oh, you are not in the beach then?" he asks.

"No, I managed to find an apartment its wonderful."

We have arrived back to the alley that leads to the spiral staircase, Jessy pulls me to him and kisses my forehead, then my nose which makes me giggle then my lips.

"I had a great day today with you," he tells me with a longing for me to reciprocate the feeling. I smile and kiss him. Followed by a wink.

"See you tomorrow maybe," I say cheekily, and Jessy smiles back at me.

"Breakfast?" he quizzes.

I gladly respond, "8 a.m." Before I know it, he is off back to his tent. I sigh with contentment as I walk through the alley to the stairs. All dark around me then the security light comes on and makes me jump and squint as it must be powered by the sun it's so bright. It's a blessing as it shows me the way to my door. I pull my key from my pocket, open the door and lock it behind me. The place is a bit of a mess, strewn with half unpacked clothes,but nonetheless I can see my bed. I find my bed clothes a simple white vest and shorts, quickly change and sink into the comfort of the bed.

As I close my eyes, I remember the sensation of the kiss, the touch of lips, and as I relax into the sensual memory I drift into a deep sleep.

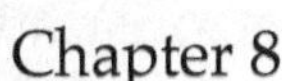

Chapter 8

Happy Fifteenth Birthday

I peak through the gap of the door into the lab. I can hear voices but ones I have not heard before.

The Director of the Institute Dr. Stephen England joined the Sanctum in the early eighties and has been the Director for over twenty years. He has an extensive background in Neo Natal Care and In-veto fertilisation. Older in appearance than he actually is. He Looks like he could use a good meal, very thin for such a tall man. Very imposing in his height at six feet and four inches. But has a look of smart military look about him, clean shaven, clean crisp shirt and tie.

He is talking to two men; one in a navy-blue suit young face, tall and good looking but dark under the eyes, like he needs to eat more vegetables. The other man is older, dressed in a uniform of some kind. Dark green and lots of badges. He stands so straight, and I giggle to myself that his clothes have no creases he must find it hard to move in his clothes. It makes me itch, instinctively scratching my behind just thinking about it.

I listen closely, the Director is not happy. I hear his voice sternly saying, "But we are moving forward with Project Preaditus." He continues, "So far the progress we have made is beyond monetary value, years ahead in research and advanced bio-genetics and beyond the current capabilities of any other nation. we have wiped out eighteen drug cartels alone in the last twelve months, terrorist attacks have been stopped, and all from the work here, we have located more terrorists on the most wanted target list than any other agency'." His voice reaching a strained pitch through his teeth in his anger. "311y has in only four years advanced from reading thoughts, to assimilating language skills plus retaining them post the connection and we have seen glimpses of mind control being able to change memories."

The Director tries to continue and the man in the uniform General Page holds his hand up and says, "Enough."

"But General Page, Sir," says the Director.

The general interrupts, "If we are going to continue to fund this from our budget then I want to see the subjects, especially 311y." I gasp and quickly put my hand over my mouth so that I am not heard. Me! why me? I ask myself.

The Director begins to shift uncomfortably and says, "She is not well today." Trying not to look at the general directly.

The general is not pleased and says, "I don't care if the subject is dying, I want to see her and I want to see her now," his voice contains a sharp tone that reminds me of Tom.

"Sir," the Director calms himself and begins to explain the situation. "We have seen a reoccurring theme with 311y that every five years her abilities evolve."

The General looks curious at the Director, "What do you mean evolve?" he asks impatiently. Turning his whole body to be mirroring the Directors. The two men listen intently to the explanation the director is giving.

"We saw at five-years old her ability to connect to the mind of others, but only understand her native tongue - English. Then we saw at the next milestone of ten-years of age where she could understand and retain all other languages including remote dialects." His tone begins to become excited as he continues, "And now at fifteen she seems to be in the third phase. We anticipate her ability to evolve to being able to remove thoughts such as the present where we interrogate criminals." The Director at this point is quite excitable and has a big smile across his face with pride of the developments that has just been explained.

There is a pause whilst the General takes in the information that has just been relayed. "I still want to see her and observe what she can do," he states in an authorative tone.

It scares me and I rush back to my bed.

My head is pounding, and I can only just open my eyes the light hurts. It's happening again I tell myself. I pass out as the pain is so intense that I can't bear it anymore.

I wake suddenly, and before long the noise outside of my room is distracting me from my own thoughts. What is the commotion that I can hear? I hear lots of footsteps and hurried movement, what is going on? its so out of the normal and usualhustle and bustle of activity. This noise is frenzied, out of control and it sounds bad.

I call out, "Oscar are you there?" Mum can you hear me?" In seconds they appear.

"Oh darling I'm so glad to see you awake, how are you feeling?" she asks.

"Hungry," I say smiling at her. She turns to Oscar and tells him to go and get me some toast and let the director know that I am awake.

"Elly what do you remember?" she asks.

I look at her and very confused. I ask, "What's wrong?" I had one of my headaches and like always I went to sleep."

I add, "It was really pounding this time, not like I have felt before though."

She looks at me smiles and calming herself she tells me, "You have been unconscious for five days Elly." I can't believe it, surely that not right.

"But why?" I ask confused.

She shrugs her shoulders and reassuringly she tells me, "That's what we need to find out. was the headache worse than before?" she asks.

"Yes," I add. "What do you think this means?" I say looking worried.

"I am not sure darling, but you know that we will need to test you and see what has changed."

I slump back into my pillows more tests. "Do we have to?" I say.

Before she can reply in bursts the Director and Tom. "Ah you are awake 311y," says the Director who never calls me by my name. He turns to Tom and asks, "Have you a subject in the lab for 311y to test?"

"Yes sir," Tom replies.

"I am not doing it," I say like a petulant child.

"WHAT!" exclaims the Director.

Trying to calm the Director, Mum steps in "Elly has just woken and needs food and a check over her vitals before we can proceed," looking over to Tom for agreement. He jumps in.

"Yes, Sir we can review her vitals and then look to perform some tests maybe in a couple of hours," staring at me. I fold my arms and look defiant. Mum sits on the bed and as she puts her hand on my arms, she gently urges me to unfold them.

The Director tries to maintain his composure but is clearly annoyed. Barking out his orders he shouts, "You have one hour," turns and leaves almost bumping into Oscar who has returned with toast and jam and some orange juice.

"Eat up," Mum says smiling at me.

"Susan you need to get her ready," Tom says hastily as he starts to pace.

"Tom its ok, she will be ready but let's just make sure she is ok," she replies.

"I am sitting here you know," I say with a mouth full of toast. "I can hear you and I am not doing it," I say firmly.

Tom tries to speak and Mum as usual manages to stop him by holding up her hand, turns to me and says, "Sweetheart I know that you don't want to but please for me, let's just make sure that after your headache you are ok and nothing has changed?" She smiles and starts to move her head to one side trying to look me in the eye and get my acceptance.

"Just one," I say firmly.

"Yes, darling only one." She turns to Tom and tells him to get the subject ready. Tom nods and leaves the room taking Oscar with him.

"Elly this is very important," Mum says. I notice her nervousness. "I want you to understand that the work we do, that you do is vital to national security, do you understand that? And that's why we have to carry on," she looks more worried and sad.

"But why me?" I ask. As she looks up at me, she has tears in her eyes, and I have never seen he so sad or is it scared.

She composes herself and begins to explain, "We work for the US government on top secret biogenetic warfare, creating weapons in the fight against terrorism. You are a weapon," she adds.

"I can't tell you anymore darling as it's not safe to you or me," she holds my hand and smiles as she always does. She wipes away a tear that has fallen down her beautiful cheek and regaining her composure she kisses my forehead and says, "C'mon let's get ready." I go into the bathroom and brush my teeth, brush my hair and twist it into a ball putting on a band to tie it in place. As I return to the main room, she is stood waiting for me. "Ready?" she asks. I nod and make my way into the lab.

A man is sitting there in handcuffs, wearing a uniform. Army, I think, the same as the general? He is early twenties, dark- brown eyes, shaved head and has many bruises all over his face. I sit down and look at him. For a grown man he looks broken, sad, scared and in pain. I smile at him as I sense no malice no wanting to hurt me.

He smiles back and says, "Hey Elly how are you feeling?" I frown and stiffen in my seat.

"How do you know me, my name?" I say.

He frowns and looks at me shocked. "I have known you since you were born Elly, I am one of your guards."

I try to speak but under my breathe I hear myself saying, "What is going on."

Then before I know it a voice come over the speakers. It's Tom! "Elly get on with it."

I roll my eyes and look to the mirror for a moment. I want to show my annoyance but as a fifteen-year-old it just looks like a stroppy teenager.

I hold out my hand to the man sitting opposite me and he says, "I'm sorry."

He takes my hand and before I know it, he pulls me over the table and locks his handcuffs around my throat. A siren sounds and men rush into the lab with guns.

Mum comes running in from my room and is holding her hands out saying, "Ok calm down let's all stay calm." She is desperately trying to calm the room. I counted six guns all pointing towards me. "You don't want to do this," she says. "It's going to be ok Elly," she says but I think it's more for her reassurance than mine.

As I grab his hands to hold back the handcuffs from around my neck, I can read his thoughts. He has known me since I was born. He has been my personal guard for fifteen years. But he has also guarded others on the same wing. Joel, Steven, Cassie, Lizzy and Nat. All with abilities. He helped them escape, he was coming to get me out too, but my headache stopped him and that's how they discovered him. I see Joel being shot, and I am so scared but it's not my feelings it's his. I can hear lots of shouting in the room, but I can't make out what is being said it's like I have earphones covering my ears. I close my eyes and exhale. I think to myself, calm down, its ok, I repeat the mantra over and over several times. I clear the thoughts of helping them escape, I replace them with older images from several years before where they were stored in his memory and it's like I'm erasing words on a piece of paper, I clear the existence of the current memories and replace with new ones of the past.

As I open my eyes, everyone is looking to see what happens next, its quiet. He moves his hands from around my throat and says, "What's going on, why am I in handcuffs?" Joe is confused and asks, "Elly are you ok?"

I move away quickly over to where mum is standing, and he sits back down. The sirens have stopped and the men with guns leave the room. Mum is still there standing by me.

"Joe what do you remember?" she asks the man sitting in the lab. "What day is it?" she asks. Joe looks over and smiles.

"Susan its Thursday December eighteenth the Christmas party is tonight, I can't wait, are you still going?"

"What year is it?" she asks, and Joe looks at her surprised.

"2016," he replies. She turns to the mirror and nods.

"Thanks Joe, you can leave now and return to your station," she explains, another guard comes in and removes his handcuffs and they both leave the room together.

Mum and I sit down and she looks at me quizzically. "Elly tell me what you did?" she asks. "What did you see in his memories?" she asks. "Elly you have to tell me darling?" she is asking me in a way that sounds desperate.

I look at her and realise what my abilities have evolved. But also, the fact that where I am people like me are more prisoners than guests, and if I want to leave there is deadly consequences. Mum had mentioned before others but then asked me not to question this and forget it. Is this why?

She holds out her hand to me and asks me again. "Tell me what you did." I smile back and realise that I can't tell her everything as others are listening.

"I wanted to calm down as I felt scared, so I repeated over and over to calm down its ok." I added, "Then I erased the memory of today and replaced it with older memories, the first one I could find that was calming. It was like using an eraser on a piece of paper and wiping it out," I explain. She looks shocked.

Asking me, "What did you see that was current?" She is looking worried I can see that she is scared I have seen too much.

"I saw him pacing the corridors and smiling at you and dad," I said.

"Is that all?" she asks challenging me.

"Yes, mum what else could there be?" I say in a quizzical way. Trying my best to seem confused by the question. She seems to soften her pose not so stiff as if she is relieved of my answers.

"What does this mean?" I ask.

She smiles at me and says, "Not sure darling, but let's leave it there for today." she gestures me to go back into my room out of the lab. "I will be with you shortly darling," she says as I leave the lab.

Oscar appears in my room with tea and cake. "It's your birthday cake," he tells me.

I smile at him saying, "Thanks Oscar are you having some?"

"Not this time Elly but thanks," he says as he drops the tray on the bed and leaves me to it.

I can hear mum taking in the lab but pay no attention as the cake is all I can focus on as I am starving!

After a while I hear mum say, "She can change memories Tom. He will never let he go." I can hear she is worried with a scared shaky tone to her voice. "This is our daughter, our flesh and blood I don't know how much more I can put her through," she pleads.

"Susan, we have to, our lives depend on it" is Toms reply.

Chapter 9

Job Hunting

I wake suddenly, hot and tangled in my covers, it was only a memory. I look at the time its 7am, I think I have time for a run to clear my head ready for the day ahead. I scramble throwing to the side my bed covers to get to my bags and grab my running gear a pair of shorts and vest top. I quickly get dressed and I check the shorts pocket as I usually have a band to tie my hair back with. luckily, I find one. Lastly slipping on my runners, pulling up the tongue to make sure they fit snug.

I head out of the door down the spiral stairs tying up my hair at the same time in a knot on top of my head. I start heading to the beach, the boardwalk I think is a great place to run and breathe in the fresh salty air at the beginning of the day. Starting with a gentle pace to warm up, I head down the road. Then once I hit the boardwalk start to pick up pace. I see a lot of runners there and everyone nods when they pass me I guess an acknowledgment of me being a runner or something like that. Plus, what I have noticed Australians are very friendly, always first to say hello or smile and give eye contact. I have noticed it everywhere I have been.

This run feels great, a warm breeze brushes over me, it's going to be hot today I tell myself as its warm so early. As I reach the end of the boardwalk, I stop and take in the view, the ocean is stunningly mesmerising all the shimmering colours reflecting the sunlight. I do some stretching as I think to myself, I need to get back, so I turn begin and run back the way I came.

I enter the apartment, happy and refreshed from the run, clearing away the shiver from the night terror. I make the bed then pull out some clothes for today. I think to myself it's going to be warm, a pair of shorts and a vest will suffice. I find my cut off denim shorts, black bikini and plain black jersey vest as I am sure I will end up at the beach at some point in the day. I lay them on the bed and switch on the shower. I undress and scoop up any remaining clothes strewn on the floor and put then into the washing machine. A quick cleansing shower and I start to get ready.

A loud knock on the door startles me. "Hannah, it's me" Jessy calls through the door. "You're late," he adds.

It makes me smile I look over to the clock on the wall its 8.30am but he's not mad. I go to the door and open it. He is standing there in a pair of khaki cargo shorts, a white t-shirt with a smile that is to die for. Unshaven today with a wisp of dark hair all around his mouth and chin covering the beautiful golden tan he has, the glow from the white t-shirt make the tan seem more evident, he is so handsome. I tell my inner self, "Stop staring"! Then realise I am in just a towel!

"Hey, you," he says with that award-winning grin. I am just in awe and smile without being able to say a word. After a pause he asks, "Can I come in?"

"Oh, my goodness yes of course," I say realising I have just been standing there staring at him. "Erm, I won't be long ten minutes and I will be ready. is that ok?" I ask.

"Sure, take your time," he says. As I close the door behind him, I grab my towel holding It tight making sure it doesn't fall.

"Make yourself comfy," I say waving my hands all around the apartment. I rush over to the bed and grab my clothes and head into the bathroom closing the door behind me.

I look in the mirror and see this stupid grin across my face and roll my eyes at myself! I brush my teeth, dry my hair and tie it back in a knot and get dressed. Final check in the mirror turning from one side to the next to see if everything looks ok. I nod to myself in the mirror and open the bathroom door. I quickly jiggle as I am putting on my flip flops and I smile at the thought of Aussies calling them thongs!

Jessy is sitting on the end of the bed with his hands interlocked resting his forearms on his thighs. "Nice place," he says immediately as he sees me.

"I love it," I reply without any hesitation. "Shall we?" I say as I walk towards to the door. Jessy stands and comes over to me. I stretch out to open the door and he grabs my hand pulls me towards him and kisses me. I respond immediately and throw my arms around him. I am so energetic from having the run earlier.

As our kiss breaks and we part regaining our composure. Jessy pipes up, "Well that is a hell of a good morning," while running his hands through his hair, noticing its looking more golden today than the usual dark brown with flecks of light blond colours.

"Let's eat, I could eat a mountain," I say. I open the door and gesture him to go through. I lock the door behind us and we both make our way down the spiral stairs.

"Can we eat here?" I ask Jessy as we walk through the alley to the main street. Pointing out the café.

"Sure, I like it here," he adds.

The familiar sound of the bell chimes once I push open the door, we enter the café. Its 8.30am and its really busy. Pamela seems a little stressed as she is not her usual smiley self.

"Be with you in a sec doll," she pipes up.

"No worries," I reply and look around for a seat. "where shall we sit?" I ask Jessy.

"I can see a table at the back," he replies.

So, we head over weaving our way through. It's a hum of noise as everyone is chattering and eating, clattering cups on saucers and clinking of spoons stirring coffee. Whooshing of the coffee machine as it heats up the milk and the smell of fresh ground coffee and bread fills the air.

Pamela comes over, "What can I get ya today?" she says half smiling wiping away her hair from her forehead with the back of her hand. She always looks the same in the last three times I have seen her. Jeans and T- shirt with a denim apron, her curly red hair tied up with a flowery bandana wrapped around like a hair band. Her hair is unruly as the curls look natural.

Jessy looks at me and waits for me to order first. "Erm, two poached eggs, on sourdough toast with a side of bacon and mushrooms please," I order.

Jessy looks at me. "Hungry?," he says cheekily. I smile sweetly back at him and wait for him to order.

"May I have the full breakfast please?" he asks.

"Sure doll, what drinks for you both?" Pamela asks scribbling down our order on her pad.

"Coffee for me please." I say, "Flat white," by way of explanation.

"Tea for me please." Jessy adds, "A nice strong English Breakfast if you have it?"

Pamela winks at him, "Sure do doll." The door chimes and she look over. "Grab a seat and I will be with ya in a sec," she shouts over to the entering customers. "Is that everything?" she asks and we both nod.

"Is everything ok?" I ask, "it seem really busy, are you on your own?" I ask.

"I'm fine," she says, and she grabs and squeezes my hand, "Thanks for asking doll." And off she goes to put our order into the kitchen.

Jessy frowns at me looking puzzled. "What's up?" I say.

"Do you know her?" he asks me.

"Not really," I say. "But you know good people when you meet them," I say by way of explanation. Giving him a cheeky smile and wink. He just sends his charismatic smile back and I know I am blushing by the warmth I feel in my cheeks.

Our meal arrives amidst clashing from the kitchen as it sounds as though the cook has thrown all the crockery on the floor. Pamela just rolls her eyes and smiles and goes to see what is going on.

We eat our breakfast and it just hits the spot. Jessy pipes up, "What do you want to do today?" he asks.

"Well I need to find work, Girl can't live on her holidays forever" I say with a shrug of my shoulders.

"Ok so what are you looking for? what type of work have you done before? What experiences can you offer?" he asks. I feel uncomfortable as I know he is trying to help but I am also not prepared for this, what do I say. What if they catch up with him, the more he knows the more he is in danger! My mind drifts back to Duke. I hope he is ok.

"Ok Ok," I reply hastily. "Not sure what I want to do, it's just for money to live on." I add, "Travelling the world on a budget isn't easy," and as I look at him and just smile hoping for acceptance of my explanation. "Let's go for a walk to work off the breakfast and see what adverts are in the shop windows," I say, breaking the silence and throwing Jessy off his torment of questioning.

Jessy nods and we start to move off. I notice though how stretched Pamela is and pick up our dirty plates from our table and take it to the counter, picking up a few other tables dishes too. I nod to Jessy to do the same and he obliges immediately.

"Hey thanks doll," Pamela says as she is rushing out of the kitchen with another order.

"No worries," I reply. "Would you like me to clear the rest to get you on track?" I ask and she looks at me pauses and then nods with relief.

"C'mon Jessy lets help out for a moment," I tell him and without hesitation he starts clearing tables with me. As I take the next set of dishes back to the counter, I notice a cloth and detergent so pick it up and wipe down the tables that we have cleared. Jessy takes the dishes into the kitchen and loads the dishwasher. In no more than ten minutes we have finished. I turn to Jessy and say, "That's our good deed done for the day." he nods with agreement.

As we leave the café, "Thanks," I hear behind us as Pamela is serving another customer. I wave and look back to see Pamela looking a little more relaxed.

"happy to help, just shout if you need anything," I reply.

Turning back to Jessy, "We worked well in there," I say. "I think though you may have done it before," I say with a quizzical tone.

"Yeah, waiting tables was my mainstay throughout uni," Jessy tells me. "It paid for the beer," he says laughing. "My parents paid for the tuition until." He stops abruptly and a pained expression appears on his face as if a secret that was buried has now resurfaced. I know that feeling only too well.

As we walk towards the beach and the main shopping area Jessy walks with his hands in his pockets quite stiffly it appears, all straight arms but a little bouncy in his step. We are silent an awkward silence waiting for a new subject in our conversation to break the silence.

"I found my apartment from an advert in the newsagent window let's try there first," I say breaking the silence between us, and looking for acknowledgement from Jessy.

"Sure," he says with a smile and we head down the main street.

After a couple of hours of job hunting and the high number of people we have spoken to. I suggest to Jessy, "We have been at this for hours shall we have a break? let's go to the beach!" I say excitedly. He looks at me and still has that pained expression but nods in agreement.

I quicken the pace, "C'mon slow poke," I say teasing him. "Race ya," I say biting my bottom lip waiting to see if I can bring him out of his deep thoughts. He raises an eyebrow and before I know it, he is off racing towards the beach. Wow he is fast I chase after him, but I can't catch him. We arrive at the beach and both of us panting short of breath laugh.

"So what's my reward for winning?" he asks cheekily sounding a little more like the playful Jessy.

"First prize a kiss," and I lean in to kiss him. He responds with a passionate kiss and for a moment the world stops spinning and all that is here and now is the kiss we are sharing.

As we break apart Jessy says, "First prize eh, I like it," and we both laugh.

It's very warm the temperature, I would guess is around thirty degrees celsius and the gentle breeze coming off the sea is a welcome one. We find a spot near to the water and Jessy sits down. I look at the water as it's so tempting and start to remove my vest and shorts. I am standing in from of Jessy in my Bikini. Looking at him he is sitting there with his mouth open just staring.

"What's wrong?" I ask.

He composes himself swallows hard and says "Nothing," in an uncomfortable voice with a higher pitch than normal.

I look at him for a few seconds to see if I can gauge what's up with him. He's not hurt or seems to be in pain I have no idea. "I'm going for a dip, you coming?" I ask.

Jessy shakes his head and awkwardly says, "no you go."

So off I go, the water feels amazing its cooling and refreshing. I look for Jessy on the beach and wave. He waves back and after about twenty minutes I head back towards him. I stand in front of him all glistening from the water and he stands up and we are nose to nose.

"you are so beautiful," Jessy says in a slow hushed tone. I feel his hands stroking my arms and he rests his forehead against mine.

It's confusing as I am lost in the emotions that I feel. What does it mean? I am happy, and feel a way that I have never experienced before. Its scaring me but not enough to make me stop. I close my eyes and let the feeling wash over my whole body.

"Let's head back," Jessy says. "You will need a towel." As I nod with agreement, I put on my shorts and vest as we head off back to my apartment.

It's just after lunchtime and I can see in the café it's still very busy. I say to Jessy that I need to go and get changed, clean up and thank him for his company today. He takes the hint and steps back, "Can I see you later?" he asks.

"Errm, I have some things I need to do but how about breakfast tomorrow that would be good?" I say by way of suggestion.

"OK," Jessy replies but still seems off in some way. I take his hand and look into his eyes.

"Are you ok?" I ask, "You seem very upset when you mentioned uni," I add.

He is looking uncomfortable and raises a half smile not his usual blow you away smile and says, "yeah, I'm ok."

I lean over, kiss him gently and say, "I don't need to know only if you want to share, I will listen," I tell him. I squeeze his hand and let go.

He looks at me and pauses before he replies, "I have never met anyone like you Hannah, and I am glad I have now." He smiles and begins to walk away back towards the bus stop, and I think his tent.

I watch until I can see him in the distance and decide to go into the café.

The door chimes as usual and Pamela looks over. "Hey doll back so soon," she pipes up, carrying a heap of plates back towards the kitchen.

"Can I help?" I ask. "You look really stretched, it's the least I can do," I add. Before I know it, Pamela has thrown over a denim apron. I quickly put it on and start to clear tables, and smiling at customer, asking them if they need anything else. In next to no time the last customer is heading out of the door and Pamela is starting to clear up ready for closing. So, I follow her lead, collect all the water bottles, clear the condiments, it's just like working at Dukes.

Once we have stacked up the chairs and the floor are mopped. It's time to head out. As I start to take of the apron Pamela is in front of me handing over a folded bunch of cash and says, "Thanks doll you are a life saver."

"There's no need," I reply blocking her hand with the cash. "It's the least I could do you have been so kind to me, and I really appreciate it," I reply.

"I insist," Pamela says. "You need it and Its only right."

I smile and know there is no point arguing I can see the steely determination in her face. "Thanks, but I helped you because you needed it not for money," I added.

Pamela looks at me and as she smiles, she tells me "I know doll its very kind of you and I knew when I first met you that you were genuine, honest and someone I can trust." As we begin to head out, she turns to me and says, "Do you want a job?"

I look at her excited, "Really?" I ask.

"Sure three days a week suit ya to start with?" she asks.

"Yes, yes, anything that would be great!" I say, and I can't contain my excitement and throw my arms around her giving her a big hug.

"Ok doll that's enough," Pamela replies as she looks decidedly uncomfortable with the hug. "We will start day after tomorrow 6am ok?" she asks. I nod in response and wave goodbye as I head into the alley to go to my apartment.

As I climb the stairs and unlock the apartment door, I stand in the doorway and look around me. I make a memory of this lovely place saying to myself. "This is the start of something really good, I can feel it."

Chapter 10

The Letter

8am on the dot, I begin to open my eyes. As I gather focus and look around, I feel happy and contented. As I begin to wake up properly, I think to myself that I want to tell Jessy the good news! I throw the covers back, jump out of bed and head into the shower. Once I am dressed and with a quick tidy of the bed I hurry out.

As I pass the window of the café, I see Pamela. Odd as its closed today, I think to myself and wave but don't even wait for the response and I am walking at a pace as am so excited to deliver my news.

Once past the bus stop, I continue down the lane my pace quickening with each step to the field, then I stop. This can't be, am I at the right place? I look around and I know that this is the spot but no tent which means no Jessy! Tears pool in my eyes as I feel so lonely and confused. Where could he be? I ask myself.

I compose myself and begin to look around travelling further along the road to other fields to see if he has moved to another field. Nothing, I begin to head back to my apartment and start to wonder if I had done anything wrong, was it the conversation yesterday about his Uni? or worse? I feel a chill and think what if the Veritas team have found him. No way could they know anything it's been three days! I shake my head as to rid it of silly childish thoughts.

I head back past the café and I see Pamela in the window she waves, I don't wave back and I just head back through the alley up the stair to my door. As I open the door, I see an envelope marked Hannah. I look and ask myself was it there before? As I left in such a hurry that morning, I have no clue.

I pick it up rushing inside kick the door behind me to close it and sit on the bed. I frantically open the envelope and see its from Jessy I begin to read aloud

Dearest Hannah

Since I have met you, I have been beside myself as you are like no-one I have ever met before. You are in my every thought.

There are many things about me that I can't tell you, it's not to be mysterious but it's because I don't have the answers myself. The answers are what I am looking for.

My journey is to find my biological parents but so far all I have found is lies, deceit and misery. I care too much to burden you with any of this.

Please forgive me I didn't mean to hurt you.

Jessy xoxo

As I read the last words tears fall uncontrollably and splash on the paper.

I drop the letter and rush out of the door, head down the staircase to the alley. As I reach the main street I run into Pamela and nearly knock her over.

"Hey doll, where's the fire?" she says. She looks up at me and sees my tears streaming down my face. She grabs my arms and asks "What happened doll?" she is stiff and tense with concern, I just slump into her and sob she puts her arms around me, stroking my head. "It's ok, it's going to be ok let's go and get a cup of tea." She says in a quiet voice that sounds so genuine and sincere.

We head over into the café as Pamela unlocks the door put the lights on. We head in. "Sit down doll and I will get us some tea," she says with a smile. I sit down and sniff wiping tears from my cheek and using the back of my hand to wipe my nose.

It's not long before Pamela is back to the table with tissues and a tray holding a pot of tea and two cups. As she pours us both a cup, she looks at me tilts her head to one side smiles, hands me a tissue and asks, "Tell me doll what's happened?." I wipe my tears and blow my nose and taking a deep breath I look up and begin to explain.

I tell her about the letter, she smiles and squeezes my hand reassuring me by nodding and smiling to the explanation I give.

I ask her, "why am I so upset? I have only just met him, and I don't really know him?" I ask Pamela confused by my emotions and not knowing what is happening.

"Oh, doll don't you know?" she asks. I shake my head. She laughs. "You are in love with him doll," she says. "I saw it when you two were in here, you looked relaxed, happy and so did he, it was lovely to see doll," she said.

"What do I do?" I ask, "I have never felt like this before."

As I look at Pamela for guidance, she squeezes my hand again and she replies, "What do you want to do?" she asks.

I pause and sit back in the chair. Pamela is pouring the tea and hands me a cup. "Doll you make your own choices as you have to live with them," She says, "My only advise would be don't' live with a regret."

I take a sip of tea and it's just what I needed. It reminds me of sitting with Mum and being able to talk about anything and everything without criticism or judgement. Just loving responses and encouragement. The thoughts make me smile, and I begin to relax.

"Thank you," I say to Pamela. "I don't know what I have done to deserve such a friend as you, but I am so grateful I really am," I say. Pamela looks at me and I can see tears pooling in her eyes, she smiles.

"We all need help from time to time doll and it just so happens that your help needed is something I can give," she adds.

"I don't know what to do, I have never felt this way before," I tell her and explain about the time I spend with Jessy and when he kissed me how I wanted him to do it again.

She laughs aloud, "doll you have got it bad," she says. "Sounds to me like this is your first love?" Pamela looks for a reaction from me.

"I guess so," I add.

As we finish our tea Pamela asks me again, "So doll what are you gonna do?"

"What can I do?" I ask. "I don't know where he is," I say.

Pamela stands winks at me, "You clear the tray doll to the kitchen, and I will be right back," she says. She hurries out of the café and I do as she asked. I sit back at the table and five minutes later I hear a truck pull up outside the café. The door opens and Pamela pops her head in, "C'mon doll", she says gesturing for me to come with.

Pamela turns out the light and locks the door to the café and there in front of us is an old-fashioned truck, Chevy P100 bull nose in a magnificent pearlescent red. "Let's see if we can find him eh doll," says Pamela with a big smile nodding her head waiting for me to give her the green light.

I look at her and the truck and I start to get excited. "let's do it," I shout and we both get into the truck. Its immaculate cream leather interior, bench seat and the biggest steering wheel I have ever seen.

Pamela turns to me and says, "I have wanted a reason to take this out for a drive doll, let's go," she says all excited and giddy.

"Where shall we go?" I ask.

"Let's head towards Berrington," Pamela advises. As we head out the truck roars into action, it sounds like a growling tiger, guttural and deep. I watch carefully as Pamela accelerates through the gears taking command of the stick' and we pick up some speed.

Its roughly thirty minutes to get to Berrington and during the drive we both sat quietly, both anxious I guess looking all around us surveying each side of the road and hoping to see Jessy. But I have no idea what I will say when I see him! I just know I have to see him.

We arrive at Berrington and Pamela says, "let's go to the bust terminal and start from there." I nod as that's a great idea. As we drive through the town, we get looks of passers by staring at the truck, I am not sure if it's the look or the sound but it's quite unnerving. We reach the terminal and park up. I jump out of the truck and we both head into the terminal. I explain to Pamela that I am going to check out the arrivals/departure boards and she nods and explains she will have a look around.

I can see that there is an arrival in ten minutes and the bus had a pickup at Terra Hope. I look for Pamela who is coming back towards me.

"I can't see him in here," she says. Shrugging her shoulders.

I point to the arrivals board. "There is a bus coming in that has picked up at Terra Hope and should be here in ten minutes," I explain with excitement in my voice, although am not sure whether it's just hope!

The tannoy announces the arrival of route ten, this is the one we have been waiting for. I rush over to the windows and see the bus coming to a stop, the doors open, and I watch each passenger as they disembark. NO Jessy! I put my hand on the glass and my head drops, tears pool and begin to fall. I wipe the tears and turn around standing behind Pamela I see Jessy.

He is staring at me looking in pain, miserable but fixed and not able to move. I am in shock that I can see him. I found him but what now? I don't know what to do. Pamela is looking at me and I can see her frowning looking puzzled, she has no idea that Jessy is behind her. She waves to me to come over to her. I can't move, my feet are lead weights.

I hear her saying, "you ok doll?" but I can't move. Jessy blinks drops his bags and begins to walk towards me passing Pamela.

He stands in front of me. "What are you doing here?" he asks.

Tears are streaming down my face and all I could say was, "I needed to see you."

Jessy runs his hand through his hair and steps forward he grabs me and pulls me into his arms, holding me tight I sob and pull him as close to me as I can. I whisper through my sobs, "I think I have fallen in love with you."

The drive back to Terra Hope was quiet with the exception of the roar coming from the truck. The bench seat meant that Jessy and I were in each other's arms and my head rested on his shoulder. We arrived back outside the café and Jessy and I got out. I ran to the driver's side and went to see Pamela as Jessy got his bags from the back of the truck.

"Thank you," I said to Pamela.

She smiles and tells me, "Go figure it out." As she drives away, Jessy is standing there at the entrance to the alley, I walk towards him and we go to the apartment.

As we sit down on the bed Jessy can see his letter on the bed, he sighs a pained sigh and says, "Hannah I am so sorry, I didn't want to hurt you, but I still did!" he says.

He puts his head into his hands. I gently slid my hands into his and lower them from his face. I look into his eyes and see tears pooling, I instinctively put my hands on his cheeks and pull him to me, our lips touch and a gentle kiss erupts into passion. He gently runs the back of his knuckles over my cheek and tucks a strand of hair behind my ear.

Stoking my face with his knuckles he starts to kiss me again. As the kiss deepens with intensity, he begins to move, he leans over me making me lean back. He continues to move with each kiss and intensity increasing, he has both his forearms either side of my head. One of his hands is stroking through my hair, he stops and I open my eyes, my chest is pounding with excitement and my breathing is fast.

"You're so beautiful," he says and kisses me again with intensity that is building getting quicker and every time our lips part for air we both murmur a moan of pleasure.

He scootches himself over to one side resting on his elbow. He raises his forearm, his hand begins to move pushing my hair away from my neck. He starts kissing me gently then he moves downwards over my lips, nipping at my chin. I lift my head instinctively and he begins to kiss my neck. Firstly, he is right in the centre then he moves again, I feel his knee pushing in between my legs. He uses his knee to push himself up and he is now directly over me. He continues kissing my neck and moves to one side under my ear. The sensation is intoxicating, and I move my head to give him more access.

As I do this his hand begins to move and it travels over my shoulder skimming my breasts that make my breath hitch, I can feel a smile appear on his face and he continues to kiss my neck. His hand reaches my waistband and I feel my body tense. I think he senses it too as he stops briefly then travels to my back and pulls me towards him.

We are nose to nose, and I have electricity coursing through my body almost paralysing me, but I am entranced by the sensation, and my desire for more is overwhelming.

Jessy is looking at me with a look that I have never seen before it's not lust, it looks more like concern in a caring way.

I have never been this close to a man before in this situation. I smile as I realise, he is the first boy I have ever kissed.

"What's so funny?" Jessy asks.

"You're the first boy I have kissed," I say. "I like it," and I let out a giggle.

"Glad to hear it," he replies.

I feel brave so I roll over and push Jessy onto his back. I climb on top of him and stroke his hair off his forehead, leaning in to kiss him I feel his hands on my back pulling me in tight to him. He scrunches my shirt with one hand and the other working its way to the base of my head scrunching my hair holding me in place as our kiss intensifies. Jessy shifts beneath me and hooks his leg over mine and rolls me over. He pulls himself up and takes off his t-shirt. I blink as it was unexpected. But his upper body is muscular, tanned and very little hair. I noticed the hair from his navel disappearing into his trousers. I like it. He takes my hands and lifts me to a sitting position. He is watching me intently and begins to undo the buttons on my shirt. After the last button is undone, he kisses the end of my nose and his hands gently begin to push the shirt off my shoulders. I shake my arms letting the shirt fall behind me, revealing my naked breasts.

"You are so beautiful" Jessy says. I lean back and Jessy follows.

I lift my hands to Jessy's shoulders and begin to stroke over his shoulders and down his arms. Jessy is kissing my neck and the sensation is so intense I close my eyes enjoying the sensation and feel Jessy's caressing and kissing move down off my neck over my shoulder then the top of my breasts. I feel myself lifting to his lips wanting more. My hands begin to grip his arms pulling him tight to me. As he moves down my hands move higher. He reaches my nipple, it hardens and as he clamps his lips over it. I moan with pleasure. I feel his tongue running back and forth over my nipple and his mouth sucking from base to tip elongating my nipple sending the most divine feeling all through my body. My hands are entangled in his hair, gripping tightly. He continues on both my nipples and I am locked in the sensations my body rising to each touch. His fingertips gently move along my side almost too sensitive a touch and hooks his fingers under my waist band. He deftly undoes the buttons and I assist by lifting my behind.

Before I can blink, he has pulled off my shorts and panties and is undoing his buttons on his jeans. As his jeans come off so does his underwear and he is standing before me totally naked. I lift up on my elbows and look at him. His body is so inviting, the hair I noticed stretches down to his penis now big and hard. He has perfect symmetry in his body and an amazing v shape from his hips that highlight his toned abs.

He moves back towards me opening my legs with his and he lowers his head and I feel his tongue travelling down the centre of my body running across my panty line. He stops and looks at me, I can't take my eyes off him. He rolls to the side and kissing my shoulder, he pushes himself against me. He asks me, "Does that feel *nice*?"

I respond breathless, "Yes." He kisses me with passion and urgency, and I respond with the same urgency. I can't get enough of this.

His hand begins to travel, and I feel it travel down over my breast. I hold my breath as he moves between my legs and inserts a finger. My hips move as my body arches with my head tilting back. I moan and exhale. He moves his finger over my clitoris and inserts it back again. He does this several times more and the sensation is building it feels amazing and I am getting lost in the feeling then he stops.

He checks for my acceptance I raise my hips to push against his hand he takes one of my hands and wraps it around his hard penis. Holding my hand in place he shows me how to caress his penis in the way he likes. He returns his attention to me and begins his rhythm again inserting and circling my clitoris, as he quickens his rhythm so do I. I can't help myself as the sensation builds my body moves with his rhythm. He adds more intensity by sucking on my erect and hard nipples. I hear myself "yes, yes, yes." And then I moan with each touch of my clitoris and I hear Jessy with every caress of his penis his breath is harder and harder.

We mirror each other and as my sensation builds to a point that I can't take anymore I cry out "Jessy," and feel my whole body shake in waves of sensation. Jessy lets out a long groan and grabs my hand and makes me squeeze the top of his penis stopping him from coming. I lay back on the bed lying still as the electricity is still running through my body. Jessy moves away and I hear him moving about. I hear ripping and then he is back. He opens further my legs with his knees. As I open my eyes his penis is still erect, and he has put a condom on. He asks me if I am ready and I nod, I am not sure I could speak at this point. As he rests his body on mine, I feel his hand searching for where to insert his penis. Before I know it, he thrusts inside me that makes me wince.

He stills himself and checks, "You ok?"

I nod again. He begins to move, in and out, slowly, he is kissing my chin and moves to my lips. He starts to kiss me, and the intensity of the kiss matches the rhythm of his movement. His pace is building faster and faster, the sensation I felt before is beginning to build again. I lift my hips and move matching his movements, it's as though we are in tune with each other's body. I tilt my head back as I begin to moan and I can't help myself.

"Yes, yes," and Jessy's head is next to mine I can hear his breath in my ear. His breathing is fast and as our rhythm hits a peak, I explode with a sensation that fills my whole body.

We lie still for a moment allowing the electricity to pass and then Jessy pulls himself out of me and rolls to the side. We lay there silent for a short while listening to our breathing return to normal. He gets up and starts fidgeting around, I can't open my eyes I am still feeling the sensation all over my body but its fading.

As Jessy climbs back onto the bed, I open my eyes, smile and just as I go to speak. Jessy says, "You ok?" I just nod with a grin across my face.

Turning on my side to face him, biting my lip I say, "That was amazing. you have made me feel things I never knew existed."I giggle and am not sure if it's a giggle of insecurity, but it breaks the ice and Jessy laughs too.

He pulls me into his arms, and I lay my head on his chest. Its feels so right being in his arms. He is stroking my back and we begin to talk. "Jessy, why did you go?" I ask not daring to look at him.

He tenses and stops stroking my back. "My father and I were the best of buddies all through my formative years. he attended all my sports events, graduation and was always the man to turn to if I needed anything. Then when I applied to uni my dad wanted me to go to Cambridge as he was alumni there, but all my friends were heading to Kings College at Oxford. So, I defied him and applied on my own. But the thing was I needed my birth certificate for the records.

I trusted my mum as we shared many little secrets and I thought she would help me, so I asked my mum, but she said that it wasn't a good idea, let it be and follow my dad's instructions. I couldn't as I thought I knew best and so in my stubbornness I went and got a copy myself. I wish I hadn't! I found to my horror that I was adopted. I can't explain to you how much my world changed and the feeling of not belonging. It took a while for me to come to terms with it and have enough courage to ask my parents. It took my whole time at Oxford to have enough strength to face it and so I did.

I confronted my parents, who at first denied the truth but I could see it in their eyes. But there was something else it looked like shame or fear I wasn't sure. When I began to try and search adoption records, I couldn't find anything that linked to me. I didn't know what to do. I turned to my uncle and asked him for help. What I didn't know was he wasn't really my uncle.

I sat up and look at Jessy, "What do you mean he wasn't really your uncle?" I asked.

A deep breath and Jessy say, "I was abducted from my real family! My uncle was a government agent who was tasked to keep an eye on me and make sure my real parents didn't come looking for me. My uncle told me everything, showed me the file and pictures it was quite a lot to take in."

I reached up cupped Jessy's face and kissed him. He responded and we wrapped ourselves in an embrace that said so much without speaking a word. We fell silent for a moment as we held each other and before long we fell into a deep sleep.

Chapter 11

Tomorrow

Its 5am I wake up refreshed, happy and excited as I start work today in the café. I look over and Jessy looks hot! My mind recalls last night, and a smile appear across my face. I ty to move out of bed as gently as possible so as not to wake him but he begins to stir.

He opens his eyes and turns to face me. "Hey beautiful," he says trying to keep his eyes open. "Where are you off too?" he asks.

"I start work today at the café, Pamela has given me a job three days a week. Isn't that great?" I say. Jessy gives me one of those Jessy smiles and I beam back at him.

"Sure is Beautiful," he says as he looks at me.

I get out of bed and head towards the bathroom. "I am going to take a shower," I tell him. I head into the bathroom, turn on the shower to let it warm up.

It only seems moments and Jessy appears moving into the shower behind me cheekily saying, "Yes good idea I could do with a shower." He comes up to me and starts to kiss my shoulder, his hands travel to my front, as he pulls me into him tightly, one hand moving to my breast running my nipple through his fingers and the other travelling south. As he continues kissing and nibbling my shoulder he moves to my neck I feel my legs becoming weak as the sweet sensation begins to build, Jessy pulls me in tighter, so I don't fall. I tilt my head back giving him access to my neck and I feel his erection, his hand moves between my legs to my clitoris and begins his magic. As he continues the onslaught of kissing my neck combined with arousing my clitoris, I know I am close, and my hands are outstretched on the wall I lean forward feeling the cool sensation from the wall against my cheek. The bathroom is filling with steam from the shower, I reach my climax and Jessy holds me tight so that I don't fall, As I steady myself Jessy steps out of the shower and returns to the bedroom. I am confused wondering what has just happened but within a moment he is back and in the shower behind me, I can see he has put on a condom. "Now where were we" he says cheekily as he nudges my legs apart with his knees and before I know it, he thrust inside me. I push back on him as the sweet sensation is almost overwhelming, I rest my head on folded arms in front of me and Jessy begins to pick up pace, we build together and as I cry out "YES," we both climax together. He pulls gently out of me and I turn around the cool wall on my back I kiss Jessy with passion, and he responds.

"I can't get enough of you," he says with ragged breath. He steps out of the shower, removes the condom and then joins me back in the shower. He washes me and then I wash him. I like running my hands over his body and feeling his hands on mine. This body is intoxicating, and I can't get enough.

We dry ourselves off and get dressed, brush our teeth together and it feels so natural for me. I quickly get dressed and as I put on my pumps, turn to Jessy and say, "Will you stay here?"

Jessy looks up at me with his beaming smile and replies, "Where else would I go!" I rush up to him and throw my arms around him, he spins me around and we both laugh out loud.

"I have to go but see you later," I say kissing him on the forehead. He releases me and with two fingers he touches his mouth and blows me a kiss.

I leave the apartment, rush down the stairs over the alley way and just as I reach the door Pamela is opening it. "Morning," I say chirpy and with a smile that I can't seem to get rid of.

"Oh, doll you have got it bad!" says Pamela and we both giggle. As we enter and Pamela puts the lights on, pressing numerous buttons the whole place seems to erupt with life so I put on the apron from before that I left under the counter and start to lay out the tables with menus, cutlery, condiments etc, Pamela shouts over to me, "you done this before doll?"

"Yes," I reply. Pamela looks over with a quizzical look but says nothing.

I am busily setting up the tables humming to myself almost shimmying around the tables. Once they are set and ready for the customers I go to the kitchen to see if Pamela needs any help. She has all the cakes, danish and banana breads ready for the front counter so I pick up the tray and head out to the counter. I check the Hot water unit is on and I can hear the water starting to boil, check the front counter for crockery and what needs replenishing and head into the kitchen still humming to myself. Now and again I look up and Pamela is watching me smiling and shaking her head at me. In no time at all we have got everything set up and ready for the first customer.

Pamela looks at me and says, "Well that was easy, you do know your way around the café doll."

"It's easy really, me and Duke seems to be on the same wavelength too." I stopped myself saying anything else putting my hand up to my mouth and I must look horrified.

Pamela came rushing over. "You ok doll? You've gone awfully pale," she said.

"Yes, I'm fine," I reply lowering my shaking hand.

"Who is Duke?" Pamela asks.

I could kick myself I have never slipped up like this before, what do I say? Luckily the door chimes, Pamela and I both turn look seeing the first customer of the day arriving alongside the chef Sam. Not knowing how to answer that question I try to give myself time by quickly attending to the customers greeting them welcoming them in ushering them towards a table. Sam looks at me quizzically as he passes me heading to the kitchen he stops and chats with Pamela. I glance over while I am seating the customers and see Pamela talking to him, she must be explaining who I am, and I see his nods of acceptance to Pamela before he heads into the kitchen. I tell the customers I will be back to take their order shortly. Smile and leave them to it.

As I head back to the counter Pamela smiles and says, "Saved by the bell eh doll." That tells me my slip up is not forgotten. I ask myself can I trust her. Mum said to trust no-one. But the turmoil inside me as Pamela has been so kind. She seems so genuine.

I go back to take the customer order and from then on, a steady flow of customers begin to arrive. This makes avoiding Pamela easy and we are busy. Before I know it, we have passed the breakfast rush and the Lunch rush and it 1.30pm in the afternoon. Pamela tells me to go have a break for fifteen minutes as I haven't stopped since 6am. I grab some tea and go and introduce myself to Sam in the kitchen area. My guard is back up after my earlier slip up.

"Hi I'm Hannah, sorry I didn't get chance before to say hi," I say. Sam just nods with a half-smile and carries on with his duties. I finish my tea and head back into the dining area.

I look over to Pamela and smile awkwardly still uneasy awaiting the follow up questions from Pamela, as I don't want to lie to her as she has been so kind to me, but I may have to!

"do you want to take a break for a while? I can manage" I explain.

"Nah doll I'm used to it; the rush is over now anyway," she tells me. "If you can clear those few tables I think we will be getting ready to close up." She adds, "not much trade leading up to 3 O'clock."

I nod and start to clear tables wiping down. The last customer leaves and Pamela follows behind them putting the latch down on the door and turning the sign on the door to closed.

Sam pops out of the kitchen, and Pamela tells him that we are closed, and he heads back in to clear down.

I turn to Pamela and say, "I'll clear in here." I head over to start putting the chairs up on the tables, once done I start to sweep up followed by mopping. Pamela has been totaling up the days take and tips. As I take of the apron and place it under the counter Pamela hands me $200 and the same to Sam.

"Tips," she says. Sam and I look at each other shocked. Pamela smiles and says, "looks like Hannah is a good addition to the team eh Sam, I can't remember the last time we made that much in tips."

Sam smiles and he just says, "Nope me neither."

It's been such a busy day that I haven't had time to think even about Jessy, but now all I can think of is him!

Pamela looks up as the silly grin has appeared on my face and says, "Go on doll, see ya day after tomorrow same time – Yeah?" she asks. I nod and smile and head out towards the door.

"Yes definitely, see you then, bye Sam," I shout as I head out the door.

Down the alley and up the stairs, I burst into the door and there lying casually on the bed reading a book is Jessy. Oh my god he is smoking hot. He sits up and smiles glad to see me. I rush over jump on him throwing my arms around him. Kissing him in the most seductive way I can.

"Missed me," he says once I release him.

"Yes," I reply.

"So how was your first day, tell me about it?" he asks. I am so excited I must be talking at a hundred miles an hour as Jess laughs, and gently puts his hand up and three fingers over my mouth.

"Slow down Hannah," he continues to laugh. "You are speaking so fast Hannah, I can't understand you."

I smile at him replying, "Sorry, there is just so much I want to tell you."

We laugh and I tell Jessy all about my day. We talk for over an hour just about the customers.

Jessy has not stopped smiling and he runs his knuckle over my cheek tucking a strand of hair behind my ear and says, "You are so amazing."

I frown at him, "Why do you say that?."

"You are just so captivating," he says.

I show him the tips and explain that it's the most they have made in one day.

Jessy jumps up off the bed and stands in front of me with his hands on his hips, a superman pose! He says, "I have a surprise for you." I look puzzled but also curious as to what he means. I just smile at him and wait for him to reveal his surprise. "I am going to cook you dinner," he says. I laugh out loud as I wasn't really too sure what he was going to say. He looks over to me and asks, "What's so funny?."

"I just wasn't expecting you to say that," I tell him. "so, what are we eating?" I ask.

He comes back over to the bed. "The only thing I can cook— pasta," he replies. I lie back and giggle out loud and Jess decides to start to tickle me. "Oh, that's funny is it," he says playfully. We roll around on the bed laughing and tickling each other, then need a moment to catch our breath. We lay side by side breathing heavy and our hands seem to find each other's so we lay for a moment holding hands letting out breathing return to normal.

"Right then– pasta," Jessy says with determination as he heads into the kitchen.

Earlier in the day he headed out to the local market for fresh ingredients and begins to whip up pasta with a tomato ragu. It smells delicious and I realise I am really hungry. We sit together on the floor and eat the delicious food Jessy has made.

"My compliments to the chef." I add, "It's delicious," as I continue to put mouthful after mouthful into my mouth.

We chat about the day and are completely at ease with each other. Jessy talks a lot about his sisters as he misses them. We take our bowls to the sink and we seem to be in one mind as without words we clear the dishes and tidy up the dreadful mess Jessy made; I look at him surprised as there is tomato ragu halfway up the wall…

"I know I am a messy cook," Jessy apologises!

There is no silence between us the night continues as it began with conversation all about now and nothing of the past. I am relaxed and content for the first time I have ever been in my life!

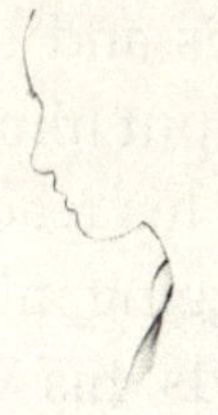

Chapter 12

Dreaming

"Don't look back," she says, and I hear a loud bang as a shot rings out.

"NO," I shout out. I sit up it was a nightmare, everywhere is dark I have tears streaming down my face, the bed is empty. Where is Jessy?

I call out and he replies, "I am here," as he switches on the lamp next to the sofa.

I squint and adjust to the light, "What are you doing over there?" I ask as I wipe away my tears. He is sitting on the edge of the sofa with his elbows resting on his thighs, fully dressed.

"You talk in your sleep," he explains. Jessy sits up a grave look in his face. My heart beats in my ears as fear rises from my stomach. "Is your name really Hannah?" he asks.

"What makes you say that?" I quiver a little, failing to keep my voice calm.

"Hannah please tell me the truth, you have been talking in your sleep," he says raising his tone not like the usual Jessy, but more pained and forceful is it time for truth I ask myself?

I look over to Jessy and he looks upset, I get out of bed and rush over to him kneeling in front of him. I look into his eyes and put my hands into his and I want to be truthful, but I don't know if I do it will I put him and me in danger.

"No," I reply. I look for his reaction, he sighs and puts his head into his hands, shrugging mine out of his.

"Who are you?" he adds, his voice quivering, He stands up and starts to pace the floor. I look down at the floor take a deep breath and stand up. "Jessy, if I mean anything to you please don't ask me anything else. Like you I am running from my past, I won't burden you with it but know that this is me regardless of what you call me, when I am with you it's the real me," I plead, looking frantically for his reaction. He looks up at me trying to gauge if I am telling him the truth, scanning my face for any reveals about what I have said.

"Jessy please believe me," I say as my voice begins to quiver, tears pooling in my eyes and not able to hold them back. Jessy looks in pain, he turns and heads to the door. "Please don't leave!" I desperately cry out. "I've never had anything like this before, I can't imagine being without you… Jessy I, I -I love you, my breath is jagged as I gasp for air, the pain a vice like grip on my heart. Jessy stops his head lowered he runs a hand through his hair, takes a deep breath and turns to face me.

"But I don't know who you are," he says softly.

"Yes you do," I reply. I slowly go towards him, I grab both of his hand and put then either side of my face with my hands holding them in place. I gently squeeze his hands onto my face and say, "You know this is truly me."

I take my hands and cup his face, gently I kiss his bottom lip. He sighs as I kiss his top lip, his hands move to resting on my shoulders. I run my tongue gently across his bottom lip and his mouth parts instinctively for me to kiss him. He pulls me into him and rests his forehead against mine. Raising a hand to wipe my tears with his thumb.

I move my head to kiss him and say gently, "Come back to bed."

He replies with, "No Hannah stop. you have to tell me what's going on."

I look up and through the dim light I can see a tear falling down his cheek. I can't lie to him…

I guide him back to the sofa and pull off a cover from the bed as I feel very awkward for some reason being naked in front of him.

I sit opposite him and leave a small distance between us. I begin the story.

"My name is 3lly, I am a genetically enhanced experiment. A lab rat. A military weapon. I lived for sixteen years in a government facility, until one of the main scientists in the facility who was secretly my biological mother helped me escape. I left USA and travelled to Hawaii, then into Australia. I am being hunted by government agents to bring me back to carry on the work I was doing before I escaped, that's it in a nutshell," I said matter of fact.

Jessy stood up started to pace the floor, incoherently he says "government, military, experiment, weapon!" I have never told anyone before so have no reference to gauge his reaction, should I have told him less I ask myself, should I have lied?

As Jessy continues to pace up and down and repeat the same words out loud, frantically trying to make sense of it all, I look at my hands and a sense of dread is washing all over me. firstly, because I have broken my promise to my mum, but also because I think Jessy will leave and I will have to move on as he may tell someone.

Through my tears that have begun again I say "Jessy," who stops and looks at me. "I am who I want to be with you," I say.

He closes his eyes and his shoulders drop as if releasing the pent-up pressure throughout his body he has been carrying.

He comes over to me and sits next to me facing me. He grabs my hands and begins to pull me to him, but I leap over and throwing my arms around him hold him tight. Although, I take him by surprise he mirrors me and holds me tightly.

His mouth whispers against my ear, "Baby I had no idea."

He leans back and cups my face kissing me with ferocious passion and urgency like never before. He throws back the cover surrounding me and removes his t-shirt. Pressing his skin against mine sending a tingle throughout my body. He stands up kicking off his flip flops and removing his shorts revealing his gloriously naked body.

I reach out and as he showed me I clasp my hand around his magnificent erection and move exactly as he showed me. He moans aloud as I increase the grip, and move forward to run my tongue around the tip, he moans louder and I run my tongue from tip to base as I guide him into my mouth. "AArrgh" he cries out as I move quicker, and his hands grab my hair guiding me to ensure he reaches his pleasure. I taste warm salty sperm as he reaches his climax in my mouth and his wholebody shudders with each and any movement. He looks down at me as I smile with a glint of mischief in his eyes.

"Wow Hannah that was unexpected," he says. "My turn," he adds playful and kneels in front of me.

He leans in to kiss me as his knees slide between my legs. He pulls me in close widening my legs, he begins to work his way across my body firstly kissing, sucking and gently nipping at my neck my head thrusts back in complete delirium as the sensations running through my body are immense.

Every breath I take exhales with a moan as every touch he makes is like a bolt of electricity all heading in one direction. As he moves further down my body kissing past my belly button, he grabs my hips and jerks me forward. He reaches my hair line and feeling his tongue work its way down mirroring the single strip of hair. He reaches my clitoris and the sensation as he circles it with his tongue makes my back arch, as my head goes back, his hands are wrapped over my thighs keeping me firmly in place. I clasp his head and my fingers begin to run through his hair grabbing it more and more as the pace quickens.

My moans are almost at a scream as all I can do is shout "YES YES YES." Then, "JESSY!," as I reach the most exquisite climax so intense that I can't move. My eyes meet Jessy's and he has the biggest smile across his face.

"Like that did you," he says playfully. He kisses me deeply and I can taste what must be me on him. I find it arousing and as I grab his head and hold him in that kiss, he grabs my thighs and pulls me to him, directing my legs to hook around him. Before I know it, he has lifted me up and I clench tightly so I can't fall. We are still locked in our kiss and Jessy walks over to the bed. As he lowers me our kiss breaks and he reaches into his bag close by and finds a condom. As he places the condom on, he climbs on top of me, holding my arms above my head, kissing my neck I arch my back and lift my pelvis up to him. He pushes against me but continues to kiss my neck. I am lost in the sensation and before I know it Jessy is lying on his back and I am on top of him. As I move my hips I can feel his erection and Jessy sits up we are nose to nose. I raise up on my knees and can feel where his erection is so lower myself gently onto him. As he fills me Jessy begins to lie back, I tilt back and forth with my hips slowly, as he lays back but once he is lying flat I begin to move up and down.

The feelings of fullness are so intense that I cant speak but moan loudly and the more pace that picks up the more the electricity increases. Jessy grabs my hips to steady me as I am losing control with each movement and it's at the point that I can't hold on anymore, I let out a loud "YES," as too does Jessy and I reach a climax together. I fall onto his chest and he holds me in his arms waiting for our breathing to calm. I roll off to the side and Jessy goes to the bathroom and removes the condom. He comes back to bed and as he slides on, he pulls me into his arms and kisses my forehead.

He strokes my back and says, "I think I am falling in love with you too!"

We drift into a deep sleep and leave the torment of the night behind.

I wake, and awkwardly I turn over as every part of my body aches. I stretch out to touch Jessy and he is not there! I panic, "Jessy, Jessy where are you?" I shout.

A click and the door opens, Jessy arrives with Coffee and Danish. "Hey Beautiful, Good morning," he says chirpily. He jumps onto the bed with a Danish pastry in his hand and he takes a bite lets out a MMMMMM and holds it for me to take a bite, I oblige accordingly. I groan a little as I move, and Jessy looks at me with concern.

"Are you ok?" he asks.

"Yes, just a couple of aches in certain places," I say.

Jessy smiles his wickedly handsome smile and replies, "Oh yes me too," and lets out a laugh.

We decide to get out of bed as crumbs are everywhere and sit at the sofa with our coffee and Danish. "We have to talk," Jessy says after a pause of silence. "We need to finish the conversation from last night," he adds looking at me for agreement.

"What do you want to know?" I ask.

"All of it," Jessy says holding his hands up expressing his need for more information.

I take a sip of coffee and sigh, "I have never told anyone what I shared with you last night," I continued. "I don't know what more to tell you."

Jessy pauses for a moment and then says, "Genetic experiment what did you mean by that?" As I look at him, I wonder if this is going to weird him out and push him away.

I explain. "I was created in a test tube, and certain genetic markers in my DNA where either removed, replaced or enhanced."

"Like what for example?" Jessy asks. I think to myself what is the simplest explanation I can give that won't freak him out. So, I think and run through examples in my head for example, I can't tell him that I was meant to be a boy, hence the 311y as Y chromosome is for male. But my DNA decided to adapt and create X female. The more I thought I could see Jessy needing some more answers.

"I have the ability to speak multiple languages," I prompt breaking the silence and tension between us. Jessy looks surprised.

"Wow that's cool, how many?" he asks. I am annoyed at myself as hadn't thought of that response.

"Erm ALL of them," I reply gingerly.

Jessy laughs. "Yeah ok, but really how many?" he asks again. I ask myself how do I answer this.

"REALLY, all of them I only have to hear a language once to be able to speak it," I say thinking that its close enough to the truth. Jessy raises his hand to rest his forehead in.

Looking shocked he says, "All of them, you can remember ALL of them?." I nod and smile trying to gauge his level of acceptance before he freaks out completely. "Ok what else?"

"Jessy are you sure you want to know?" I ask looking closely at him. He nods back to me. "What enhancements I have do not make me who I am, just what I can do, look at it like having a specific talent for a job," I say hoping he accepts the response.

"Ok," he says. I think he can see that I am uncomfortable with these questions. "So, what about growing up what was that like?" I explain about the Institute, a massive covert government facility out in the middle of the Mojave Desert, what my room was like. "So, you never met anyone else there?" he asks.

"No," I reply.

"What about your parents, do you know who they are?" Jessy asks but I can see he is getting frustrated as the answers he wants I can't give him, too much knowledge and he will be a target too. I shrug to show that I don't know but can't look him in the eye.

He stands in frustration. "Hannah, I need you to be honest with me, as I want to get to know you," Jessy says in exacerbation. As I look up, I see this gorgeous man, that I think I have fallen deeply in love with, I know I would do anything for him and this he needs to know.

"My parents are leading experts in their field of bio-genetic enhancements of embryos, they began by eradicating hereditary markers in embryos and it developed from there. They were recruited by the US Government for a specific military contract that funded their work and experiments namely ME! Susan my mother is married to Tom my father. During their work my mother used one of her own embryos and fertilized it using my dad's sperm unbeknowns to him, and created me. However, from the beginning of my life I showed unparalleled abilities even at cellular level. She never told my dad at first. As I developed, I had to perform certain test that would test my abilities, are you with me so far?" I asked Jessy. He nods and urges me to continue looking fascinated. "My dad was a beast, vile and angry."

"What do you mean?" Jessy asks with a concerned tone in his voice.

"As a child I rebelled and didn't want to do the tests, and the result of that was pain, the most brutal pain you could imagine," I explain, and every fibre of my being is reliving painful flesh memories. I try and fail to hold back tears and Jessy tries to reach out to me, making me flinch. "Jessy my dad would beat me to the point of broken bones using his hand, his belt, a stick and worst of all his fists."

He cannot hold back any longer and Jessy pulls me into his arms, and I sob as I have never before. I can feel Jessy's clenched tight jaw, saying under his breath, "A real man never hits a woman let alone a child," and hisses out, "Bastard!" I close my eyes and for the first time I feel safe. As I continue to explain staying in Jessy's embrace.

"I was just coming up to fifteen years old the last time it happened. I had four broken ribs, a broken cheek bone and my whole torso was black with bruises. My mum found them and confronted my dad, wow she was fiery! She told him at that point that I was his biological daughter. Everything changed from that moment on."

Trying to take away that memory Jessy tries to change the subject slightly asking, "Hannah tell me about your dream last night." Jessy adds, "You were re-living something." I feel myself tense and my eyes pool with tears again. "Hey hey its ok I'm sorry," Jessy says as he tries to comfort me again.

"It was the day I escaped," I tell him. "And the day my mum was killed," a tear runs down my cheek.

"Oh my god," Jessy says horrified. "What do you mean?"

"Killed for helping me escape, they shot her in cold blood," I say with great sadness. "Look Jessy I don't want to lie to you, but I don't want to put you in danger either," I tell him. "I escaped and they want me back," I say anxiously.

"OK baby calm down, its ok," he says caressing my cheek with his hand. "I will look after you, you are not alone anymore," he says and tips my head up to look into his eyes.

"Who wants you back Hannah, tell me?" he asks. As I look into his eyes, I see no evil or menace, I see sincerity.

I close my eyes calm my breathing and reply, "Veritas, a black ops division of the CIA."

Chapter 13

A Secret Shared

I can't seem to sleep after the reveals of the day and my restlessness is getting worse, my brain just will not shut off. I get out of bed and Jessy stirs a little but settles back down. A run may be my answer to clear my head so I grab some clothes, get dressed and finish by putting on my running shoes.

I head out of the apartment down the stairs and through the alley. I start to run towards the beach, its dawn and I can see the shimmering sunlight hitting the beautiful water as I reach the boardwalk. I start to pick up pace and try to expel all the regrets, pain and emotions that I have re-lived by bringing Jessy into my world. I feel my feet running faster and faster and I must be sprinting, as everything around me is a blur. I turn and head back the way I came and my pace is even quicker on reverse, I am back at the alley way to my apartment. I stop and stretch out then walk through to the staircase.

As I enter the apartment Jessy stirs, "Hey baby you ok," says a sleepy voice.

"I'm good just needed to clear my head, go back to sleep," I tell him.

He nods briefly and he falls back to sleep. I decide to have a shower and begin to undress. I go into the bathroom and close the door to not wake up Jessy and turn on the shower to warm up. I stand in front of the mirror naked looking at my body knowing that I have changed but seeing nothing different in the reflection. The shower is heating up as steam begins to fill the bathroom and cloud the mirror. I step into the show and just let the warm water wash over me. Not moving, eyes closed one hand on the wall, my head bowed, just relaxing, feeling every drop of water run down my back. I think I have been in here for a while as I hear a noise and as I open my eyes Jessy is stepping into the shower with me.

When we get out and begin to dry ourselves, I smile to myself. Jessy shouts over, "What you smiling at?," throwing over one of his socks breaking my reverie.

"Just you," I say as cool as I can manage. "How do you know how to do all that?" I ask.

"You mean sex?," replies Jessy. I nod and can't seem to stop the grinning. "I am not sure really," he replied awkwardly.

"I am not trying to put you on the spot," I say. "But the way you make my body react is wonderful and the more you do the more I want."

Jessy just looks at me and gives me that award winning smile but he lifts his chin slightly, I can see that he likes my comments I guess it's an affirmation that he is good in bed! Although, I think to myself we seem to have sex everywhere but the bed!

Once I am dressed, I kiss Jessy and head off out to the café. Same as before I arrive just as Pamela is opening the door. "Spooky!" she says "how do you do that doll?," she laughs and shakes her head.

Same as the other day we get on with setting up and before we know it, we have everything ready for the day ahead. Sam seems to be a last-minute arrival as no sign of him yet.

"Shall we have some tea before we start?" Pamela shouts over. I smile back and nod in agreement. I head to the counter and the cups are ready. Pamela looks at me and she looks awkward or uneasy.

"What's up?" I ask breaking the uncomfortable silence. Pamela looks at me and says, "I didn't mean to pry doll the other day," she explains looking for a reaction from me. I sigh and take a deep breath.

"I know and I am sorry I got all weird about it," I replied. "Pamela You have been so kind that I can't believe there is anyone before I met you that would be as generous as you have, the flat a job," I say. "I have not always experienced that in the past."

I smile and squeeze her hand as it really does mean a lot to me. She goes to say something and we both jump as the door bursts open and in falls Sam. Pamela and I look at each other and burst out laughing. Sam gets to his feet and huffs at us both as he passes us and heads into the kitchen.

"Good morning Sam," Shouts Pamela to the kitchen and we hear a grunt in response which makes us laugh out loud again!

We work through the breakfast trade, and just as it finishes lunch trade starts to make its way in, its non-stop. Every time I look over to the counter and catch a glimpse of Pamela, she seems deep in thought. Something is not right.

As the shift comes to an end, Same as before we clear down and Pamela is working through the days take and dividing up the tips. Another $200 and Sam looks at me and says, "You're good for tips."

"Thanks, I think," I say in response. He holds his hand up as he leaves waves goodbye.

Pamela turns to me, "Hannah." I look over and she looks serious, there is something on her mind.

"What's up, is everything ok? Did I do something wrong?" I say a little frantic worried I am about to lose this job.

"Let's sit doll," Pamela says and take a chair down from one of the tables, I do the same and we sit. "Do you want a cup of tea doll?" she says and tries to stand up. I grab her hand.

"Please just tell me," I say. "I can see something has been bothering you all day."

"OK doll." she sits down and takes a deep breath, as she looks at me, she begins. "You said the other day Duke." I freeze and feel panic rising. I nod as the fear is stopping me from speaking. "I know a Duke in Helen Town Peninsula." She adds, "And he has a café called Verona." I stiffen in the chair. "Is that the Duke you know?" she asks. I start to think of Duke and the last moment I saw him. I can't stop it and tears begin to fall down my cheek.

"Yes," I manage to say as I am doing everything I can to stop the floods that are coming out. I am looking down at my fingers as I feel so ashamed that Duke was hurt protecting me. The next thing that Pamela says sends the chill down my spine.

"Was it you they were looking for?" As I look up through my blurry tears I see fear in her face. I can't speak and just nod telling her it was me. Pamela gasps and puts a hand over her mouth. "Who are they doll?" she asks. I try to compose myself, but begin to sob.

"Pamela I don't want you to get hurt, I saw what they were doing to Duke and I can't bear the thought of that happening to you," I say my voice all quivering in between sniffs and sobs.

"So you called the police, Duke wondered who it was," she tells me. She puts her hand on my shoulder, "He's ok you know, more worried about you he thought they caught up with you," she said.

"Did you tell him I am here?" I ask.

"No," she says. "I said I had a customer passing through who was raving about his café." Her answer made me relax a little. But now Veritas have a lead on my direction of travel. They will come!

"Pamela, please believe me when I say these people are not good people. I am an experiment to them a lab rat not a human being. My whole life spent in what feels like a cage," I explain. "To protect you I won't tell you everything, but now they will think I have travelled through here and will come." I take my hand and cover over Pamela's hand as she was squeezing my other hand in reassurance to her. "They may already be here, when did you speak to Duke?" I ask.

"Err yesterday late afternoon," she replies shakily. "But how will they know?" she asks with her face all tight and frowning.

"Because of Duke, they will monitor to see if I get in touch. Your call will have alerted them," I tell her.

"Can I leave out of the kitchen back to the apartment?" I ask.

"Sure doll, of course," she says.

"What are you going to do?" she looks at me with concern and guilt from her actions.

"You were not to know, please don't lay this on yourself," I say. "I will need to lay low for a while, I don't expect you to hold the job and if you want me to move out of the apartment I will," I say. "Anything to keep you safe," I add.

Pamela smiles at me and says, "I am a fighter doll, and I don't give up on people especially ones who need my help- stay," she says. I hug her as this woman has not only shown tremendous kindness in my time of need but also such courage.

I say my goodbye and head into the kitchen, I hear the door chime. "Sorry Doll we're closed," she shouts out. I hear a voice a man's voice but not one I expected. It's my dad Tom.

"I'm so sorry to bother you," he says, "But I'm looking for my daughter Elly, I have a photo of her could you have a look and see if you've seen her?" he asks.

"How beautiful," Pamela says. "How old is she?" she asks.

"Sixteen in this photograph, but she will be nineteen now," he explains. "She has been missing for a while now, I'm afraid she is mentally disturbed," he adds. I can hear every word and have to bite my lip as everything he is saying makes me angry.

Pamela seems to be holding her nerve and says, "Sorry doll, no there was a young lady that passed through here about a week ago I think that looks similar."

"Do you know where she went?" he asks. "Sorry doll no, we have a few busses that come through here and my shop is the nearest to the bus stop," she tells him. "I hope you find her," Pamela adds.

They seem to leave as I hear the door chime and then being locked, followed by lights clicking off. Pamela comes into the kitchen a short while after and I appear from behind one of the tall fridges. "They have drove off," she says. I am shaking with both fear and anger. Why is HE here I ask myself! "Who is that doll?" Pamela asks.

"It's my dad," I say. "I need to show you something so that you know I am telling the truth," I add. "Come to the apartment." We leave out of the kitchen and go upstairs, Jessy looks shocked as both me and Pamela walk in.

"Hey lover boy," Pamela says cheekily, Jessy smiles and looks very uncomfortable.

I scramble for my LV as its hidden under the chest of draws on the far side of the room. I grab it and ask everyone to sit down.

Both Pamela and Jessy are sitting on the sofa, I kneel in front of them both and begin to unzip my bag. Inside there is money, ID, jewellery and photo's. I take out the photos that were in my personnel file at the institute, Mum gave it to me before I left.

"These are not pleasant to look at but show you only a brief part of the things that happened to me on a regular basis," I say and hand over the photos to Pamela. She looks horrified and at each photo she looks at, she gaps and looks over at me then passes it over to Jessy. "My dad did that," I explain. "Up until I was fifteen, he didn't know I was his daughter. Once he knew it stopped. So the man you met today Yes he is my father," I say out loud. Jessy looks up in shock.

"He's here," he says frantically.

"Yes, and he won't be alone," I say.

I feel an air of calmness wash over me as I am in the situation now and have to deal with it. So I look at them both and give my instructions! "Pamela, please I need you to go back through the kitchen and leave by the front door, in case they are watching they only see one way in and out. I am thinking that this will stop any exploring and possibly finding the apartment." Pamela nods in agreement. "Jessy you have to use this also as it will look like you are staff and no reason to question it, when coming and going. Pamela will that be ok?" I ask. "I have no choice right now. I can't run as there is too much risk they are too close for comfort, I have to wait it out and see if they are convinced I've passed through," I explain with haste.

Pamela stands, she gives me a hug says her goodbyes and makes her way out. As she leaves and looks back once I close the door behind her, listen to her footsteps down the stairs and bolt the door tight!

Chapter 14

Evade

Over the last five days its been torture. I have been held up in the apartment and Jessy has been helping out clearing tables supporting Pamela.

The good thing though is from the outward view this supports our cover story as I realised early on in my travels that the closer to the truth you lie the more believable it is. At the beginning I tried to just not say anything and keep myself to myself but that raised more suspicion. So, then I tried little bits of a story and I eventually perfected a story that was believable and the main thing was it was never challenged.

Knowing how much the Institute wants me back I assume that the café is being watched now by the Veritas surveillance team. This is the only solid lead they have had since Duke, that I think to myself they will have.

Luckily having Jessy supporting Pamela in the café means I get the full run down each day of the comings and goings. Jessy explains that my dad Tom has been into the café every day. Making idle conversation with Pamela and occasionally

Jessy. Jessy was very complimentary about Pamela as he explained She responds quite calmly but not her usual self if you knew her well. Luckily they didn't!

Both Pamela and Jessy are a little on edge, awkward and clumsy as their guard is high trying to protect me.

I'm thankful that I have two amazing people helping me hide from Veritas, but I am also feeling anxious that I can't do anything except wait. Hoping to keep myself busy and not think about everything that is going on. I begin tidying and cleaning up. I grab some of my clothes to wash and think that I can add some of Jessy's too. So I go to his bag and start pulling out clothes. As I do a mobile phone rolls out of a t-shirt that has been folded up to include the phone. I am surprised by it being hidded. Why does he have this and has never mentioned it or even used it, but more importantly why is it hidden?

I tell myself I will just ask Jessy when he comes back. But my curiosity gets the better of me and I turn it on. Its lights up straight away, when did he charge this? I press the green phone symbol and it displays one thing. Uncle Joe and he called him five days ago.

The hours are long inside the apartment. Looking at the clock I notice its about 4pm. Jessie should be finished by now. I peek out the window to see if Jessie is coming and my heart leaps to my throat. Tom! He's in the alley way, oh no there is Jessy.

I still had the phone in my hand, as I looked at the phone I realised I needed to do something so I dialled 1-300-559 it's the missing person phone line dedicated to finding me, and I leave a message of a sighting.

I race around flinging clothes into my bag as Jessy tells me what happened at the Café.

This particular morning Jessy came in through the kitchen and shouted a good morning to Pamela who looked worried. Jessy realised something was not quite right as he picks up on her body language once he reached the counter to pick up his apron, then he saw them sitting at a table in the back.

Pamela explained to Jessy that just as she had turned the sign over to open up, in walked Tom. Jessy and Pamela were both surprised and somewhat taken aback by this.

"What is there game now?" Jessy had exclaimed. and Pamela shrugged her shoulders as she has no idea. Tom was with three other men, these men surprisingly all looked the same, black pants, t-shirt and raincoats. Nothing particular that separates them in reality they could be triplets. But knowing the recovery teams that have been following me they could be I think to myself.

The door chimed and in walks Sam, nods to everyone and just heads over into the kitchen like any other day. Jessy was the one to take their order trying to act normal and not unnerved by their early presence.

"Morning Gents," he said with as much politeness as he can muster. "What can I get for you today?" He asks looking around at each of them.

Tom straightens up in his chair and replied, "Four coffees please Black."

"No problem coming right up," replied Jessy and heads back to the counter. It only took what seemed to be five minutes and Jessy returns to the table with the coffees Tom turns to him and asked, "Is that a British accent I hear?"

"Yes," Jessy replied.

"Long way from home then," said Tom. "So what brings you to this little town?" All four men turn to look up at Jessy and he felt a chill run down his spine.

As jessy swollows hard I grab hold of his hand reassuring him, but also urging him to carry on telling me everything that has happened.

Thinking on his feet and remembering what I had told him about being as close to the truth as possible he replied, "Travelling, it was always the plan once I finished at Uni, and here I am." He continued, "Started in Sydney and then over to Melbourne." Jessy smiles and returns to the counter, more customers are entering and before long the café is full bustling with chinking cups, cutlery against plates and the smell of bacon and coffee.

Jessy was busy with customers and sees Tom catch Pamela attention and gestures her over to him, before she had chance to speak Tom pipes up, "Four more coffees please."

Pamela smiles, nods and worked her way back to the counter where she is joined by Jessy she tells Jessy in a hushed almost whispered tone, "They want four more coffees," Pamela looks at Jessy and explains "looks like they are not leaving anytime soon then."

Jessy nods and takes over the coffee jug to the table. As he turns to make his way back to the counter he is questioned by Tom inquisitively asking.

"So Jessy… It is Jessy Isn't it?," Tom asks with a crooked smile on one side of his mouth.

"Yes, Its Jessy," he replied.

"So, you got a girlfriend?" Tom asks. Jessy looks puzzled and uncomfortable thinking of Hannah. But also feeling quite annoyed.

"Not really sure that's any of your business," replied Jessy and gives a firm stare back to Tom.

"Oh I didn't mean anything by it," he adds, "Its just that the cook was mentioning a pretty young thing who worked here." Jessy was taken aback by his comment and had to think fast. I suddenly felt a great dread, thinking to myself is the game up. They know and just trying to catch everyone out.

Again a quick response that flowed quite naturally was, "Must be before my time, I have only been here a week," replied Jessy he returned to the counter with the coffee jug and goes into the kitchen.

He then grabbed Pamela and told her what has just been said where they both looked over to Sam.

He looked up and said, "WHAT!"

Pamela told Jessy to go back out and clear tables otherwise it would look suspicious. Jessy pleaded to Pamela, "I need to tell Hannah."

Pamela nodded but tells Jessy "Not now, it will look odd if you disappear." She adds "I will speak to Sam." Jessy explained that Pamela wanted to get the story from Sam, let him know and we could make a plan from there. But above all we had to maintain our story or it would all be over in a flash.

So Jessy leaves the kitchen and picks up a cloth to start clearing tables as Pamela had suggested to keep up the pretence. The next thing was over came Tom to the counter on his own, "Sorry Jessy if I overstepped," he said trying to continue the attempt at small talk and lead Jessy into a conversation. By way of explaination Tom starts with, "But you see I am looking for my daughter, she is troubled and I need to get her back home safe." Tom reaches into his jacket pocket and produces a photo he showed it to Jessy. Tom asks Jessy, "Have you seen her?"

Jessy looks at the photo and then back to Tom and replied, "No I can't say that I have but as I said I have only been here a week."

Tom appeared to be satisfied with that answer and he placed the photo back into his jacket pocket. He removes some money and says, "What do I owe ya?"Tom hands over a $50 note and says "Keep the change." Then the other men stand and leave the table, walk over to the counter where Tom is standing.

Funny though, the one thing he remembered was One of the men then leans over to Tom and says in his ear but just loud enough for Jessy to hear, "Everything is ready, Sir." Tom nods acceptance and turns back to Jessy.

"Looks like we are moving on," Tom explains.

"Oh, Where to?" Jessy asks to see if he could get any indication of what they were up to.

Tom looks at Jessy and after a small pause replied, "Berrington, seems that we may have a possible lead at the bus station on CCTV." Jessy goes cold and remembers Hannah coming to meet him there, as he focuses back to Tom he sees a wry smile on Tom's face and Toms words are chilling saying, "Maybe see you around kid," and then they all leave the café together.

Jessy hastily heads into the kitchen and grabs Pamela's arm pulling her to one side. Sam looks up and frowns, shakes his head but then carries on with his work. Jessy whispered to Pamela "They know about the bus station they are heading there now."

Pamela looked at Jessy horrified then tells him what Sam has been saying, "They also know you have a girlfriend that Sam recognised as Hannah so they know she is somewhere nearby," explaining Sams part in this story. "Sam was getting drunk in the tavern last night as usual but his liquor was being bought by Tom" Pamela explained to Jessy he's a fool but he meant no harm. "That's, how they know" she adds.

Jessy explains that he decided there and then it was time to go.Pamela stops Jessy as he tries to head out to the apartment.

"Think doll," she says making him realise he was doing exactly what they wanted. She pauses for a moment, "Go now and tell Hannah to pack everything up, I think I may have a way to get you out of here," she said "GO do it now"! Jessy headed at pace out of the back door and ran straight into one of the men who were sitting with Tom.

Jessy shouted out, "What the hell?" and the sound travels back through the kitchen as the door was closing slowly Pamela heard what Jessy had said. She headed back into the kitchen and headed out into the back yard.

"What's going on?" she shouted as Tom and the three goons seems to be looking around. Tom steps forward.

"Oh sorry I think we must be lost, we were looking for a short cut."

Pamela stepped forward and firmly explained, "No short cut through here doll, this is private property so please leave," and she began to usher them all back through the alley. Jessy looked up at the apartment and could seethat I am was looking through a small window.

Tom held his hand up. "So sorry we didn't mean to cause any concern, we just got turned arounds that's all," he says. "We'll get outta your hair, C'mon on," he says to the other men. One of them touched his ear and it's the first time Jessy had noticed they all have earpieces like Government agents that you see in the movies. One of the men He whispered something to Tom and they all head out at pace. Pamela and Jessy look over at each other and they heared car doors open and slam shut followed by screeching tyres as the car pulled off at speed.

I go to the top of the Stairs to the apartment showing them I have a mobile phone! Letting them know It was me who got them to leave.

Chapter 15

Jessy and the CIA

The last piece of clothing goes into my rucksack.

After finishing his story, Jessy comes over and throws his arms around me as I think he wants to reassure me but he is far more agitated than me as I am calm. "You ok?" he asks as he senses my calmness.

I nod, "It's nothing new to me, I dread this moment but I have faced this fear for almost four years." He smiles a half smile and runs his hand through his hair.

"We need to get out of here," he says.

I look at him, "WE?" I say.

Jessy looks at me. "I'm coming with you Elly, now that I have found you I'm not letting you go," he says. I smile as he called me Elly. I ask myself can I run with him? I can't bear the thought of not being with him but I never really imagined being on the run with him!

"Where did you get that phone?" Jessy asks.

"Your bag," I tell him. Jessy looks worried.

"I wasn't snooping," I say quickly. "I was washing your clothes," by way of an explanation.

"It's ok," Jessy adds, "My uncle gave me the phone and said if I ever needed anything I could use it to contact him."

"What does your uncle do?" I asked pretending I hadn't seen the call, best to be safe.

"He works with my father in the family business," he explains.

"But if I contact him I don't know if he will tell my father where I am," Jessy adds, "Until he is ready to tell me who I am I won't have anything to do with him." He says with steely determination.

"Jessy, we have to go now," I say. "I have only given us a couple of hours before they come back," I explain.

"What did you do?" Jessy asks.

"I rang the tip line they created, supposedly a missing persons hotline and sent a tip through to their fake hotline, it's a front I know for the institute but I told them a girl matching my description was spotted in Berrington," I explained.

We grab our bags, and as usual I take a last hard look around. I really hoped this time was the last time. I only have myself to blame I got complacent and revealed too much.

We head down the stairs and Pamela greets us, she has tears in her eyes. She hugs me and Jessy and hands me an envelope. "What's this?" I ask.

"It's not much but I know it will help you," she explains. I open the envelope and its full of fifty dollar bills.

"There must be a few thousand in here!" I exclaim. "No I can't," I say trying to give it back to Pamela.

"Please take it," she says as a tear falls down her cheek, "If I hadn't rang Duke this would never of happened." she looks at her hands.

"It's not your fault," I say. "Please don't blame yourself," I add. "How could you possibly know? you have been the most amazing friend that has shown me kindness I never thought possible and I will never forget it. You took me in - a stranger and gave me a place to live, a job and became true friend, one I will always treasure," I feel myself tearing up and hug Pamela. She hugs Jessy and tells us she has an idea.

"I think I can get you out of here without being seen she says," Jessy and I look at each other hopeful and wait for the explanation. "I have a linen collection coming today for the table cloths and they should be here any minute if the last few collections are anything to go by." She continues, "If you two hide in the basket," she points to a large basket on wheels at the kitchen door, "you can leave unseen!" She sounds excited and smiles as she wipes her tears.

"Perfect," I say.

She helps us get into the basket with our bags and covers us over with the linens, I grab her hand and I close my eyes, I search her memories to where we first met. I remove all her memories after that point so that she can't be in any further danger, especially the ones of Tom. When he comes back to interrogate her he will see she doesn't know him or remember him from his last visit and know that I have taken her memories away. Seeing this I hope he leaves her alone.

I take my hand back under the linen and hold my finger up to my lips to keep Jessy quiet. Pamela is a little dazed, "What the heck am I doing here?" she says out loud. Jessy looks puzzled at me and I shake my head still gesturing him to be quiet.

"Oh, hey doll," Pamela pipes up. "It's all ready," she says and before we know it the basket is moving. I hear the kitchen door close and realise Pamela has gone back into the café. The basket is being pushed down the alley and up a ramp. The person pushing this is making strained noises as the basket must be really heavy, more than usual with me and Jess hiding underneath the linens. We stop moving and hear the ramp being pushed back into the truck plus the sound of shutters coming down and its quite dark, they must be the rear door to the truck. Engines fire up and off we go.

Jessy turns to me and says, "What happened back there?"

"let's get out of here first then I will explain," I say. I don't think he is happy with my answer but for now he lets its go.

We have been in the truck for about fifteen minutes and we stop. The shutter doors go up and everywhere becomes lighter.

"I think it's another collection," I say. After a small pause I turn to Jessy. "This is our chance to get out lets go," I say and we hurriedly get out of the basket and grab our bags.

We jump out of the truck as no ramp this time take a look around and start walking away from the truck.

"I have no idea where we are, do you?" I say and look at Jessy who doesn't make eye contact.

"Jessy what's up?" I ask.

He looks up at me and says, "What happened back there?"

"Jessy, please," I plead.

"I need to know," he says.

I shake my head and look at my feet, I take a deep breath and raise my head saying, "Remember I said that I was able to speak every language?" He nods. "Well that wasn't all," I explain looking at him for a reaction.

"I also have the ability to look into your memories and either change them or remove them," Jessy steps away from me and has a look of horror on his face. "I removed any memory of me and you from her memory to keep her safe," I add quickly.

Jessy looks up at me and says, "Have you messed with my head too?"

"No, No, of course not! Jessy please I can't with you," I say frantic to try to make him believe me.

"What do you mean, you can't?" he asks.

"At first when you held my hand yes! I could see your family your sisters that's why I shrugged you away as I didn't want to see into your memories, but then after we kissed I noticed that there was nothing," I explained.

"How do I know you are telling me the truth?" he says his voice is worried somehow.

I looked at him and say softly, "You don't, but it's about whether you want to believe me and trust me or not. I have no reason to lie to you, I have shared my inner most secrets with you and hate myself for bringing you into this world. But I love you Jessy and can't bear the thought of not being with you."

We walk for a short while, Jessy silent deep in his own thoughts. I cant stand the silence between us and blurt out, "Jessy, I know its not easy." But if you feel about me the way I feel about you then I hope you know that I am telling you the truth. If you don't feel the same then tell me now and we go our separate ways," I say searching for a reaction from him.

I look at him and wait for his reaction. "I cant bear the thought of being without you," he says quietly He steps towards me and tries to hug me but my camo backpack I always have on my front gets in the way. We both giggle and it breaks the mood.

"Let's cut across country," Jessy says. "Avoid the roads, just in case," he adds with a nod towards the road. He looks at his watch and says we have probably about an hour before we need to pitch the tent, otherwise we are sleeping under the stars.

We continue to walk pretty much in silence as I guess both of us are replaying several events of the last five days. As we climb into another field by a grand oak tree Jessy says, "Let's pitch here, the tree will give us camouflage."

"OK," I reply.

We make haste and pitch the tent as the day is drawing to an end and the light is fading. Jessy makes light work of pumping up the air bed and puts on an oil lamp so we can see. I drop my bags on the floor next to the air bed and flop onto the bed. I'm exhausted from the day's events both physically and emotionally.

Jessy lays next to me and asks, "How are you doing Elly?"

I smile and say, "Thankful."

"What for?" he says.

"YOU," I say and turn to face him and gently kiss his lips, waiting for him to respond. He does with passion and we lose ourselves in the moment.

When we break Jessy says, "We should rest and get an early start in the morning." He smiles at me but not his usual blow me away smile, he is not himself and I am curious as to what is coming next.

We settle down on the bed and Jessy is behind me and we mirror each other's body. Jessy has one arm folded under his head and the other wrapped around my waist holding me close to him. I feel safe and begin to drift off to sleep.

"I can't tell you why Uncle Joe, you said if I needed help you would give it… I have no idea where I am, you can track the phone to my location can't you?... I need help Uncle Joe I'm into something and need to move out of the area fast," I hear Jessy talking outside the tent. Its sounds like he is leaving.

"Why are you in Australia Uncle Joe? Promise me you won't tell my dad? OK text me the details, we'll head out now." I hear footsteps and Jessy must be heading back so I pretend to be asleep.

"Elly," Jessy is nudging me gently. "Wake up Elly we have to go now."

"What's going on?" I say, as I pretend to be sleepy.

"I'll tell you once we get going," he says handing me my bags.

"What about the tent?" I ask.

"We don't need it where we are going," he explains.

I freeze I'm scared of what's happening, it's out of my comfort zone I am not in control. I don't like it. I'm shaking as I feel trapped like a tiger backed into a corner. Jessy can see my demeanour, "Elly its ok. I won't let anything bad happen to you," he says. "I spoke to my uncle who is coming to get us out of here."

"Jessy I'm scared this is getting out of control, too many people involved." Jessy rushes to me and holds me close to him.

"I know you are scared," he says. "I trust my uncle. he helped me for a while before I set off travelling," he explains. "He will be able to get us somewhere safe."

I look up at Jessy and ask, "How?"

Jessy replies, "Because he is MI6!"

Uncle Joe

Once Jessy explained what MI6 was I relaxed a little, but was still uncomfortable with meeting someone new. I asked Jessy to call me Hannah not Elly in front of his uncle so that it didn't raise any suspicions.

It's just reaching dawn and Jessy has been holding my hand tightly since we left the tent, and we both stop as we see a figure in the next field, he releases my hand for a moment and I shake it to get the circulation back. We both tense up then a flashlight comes on and flashes twice. I can feel Jessy relaxing as he realises that we have found his Uncle Joe. He grabs my hand again and we head over.

Looking at Uncle Joe; six feet tall I guess, slender like my dad Tom, grey hair, grey stubbly beard and blue eyes just like Jessy's, he must be in his forties but I am terrible at guessing ages. As Jessy releases my hand again, he steps up to his Uncle Joe and they hug, manly patting each other on the back.

"Good to see you boy," says his uncle. As they turn towards me he puts one arm around Jessy.

"This is Hannah, Uncle Joe," says Jessy in a flash.

"How do you do," he responds to me and extends his hand to offer a handshake.

"She's shy uncle," Jessy pipes up and puts his uncles hand down at his side. I just smile and look at my hands rather than directly at him.

"So, the plan Uncle," says Jessy.

"Yes lets go," he replies and they both turn and still linked together start walking towards what looks like a plane.

They are whispering together but I can just make out what they are saying. His uncle is teasing Jessy of how beautiful he thinks I am and what on earth I am doing with a ragamuffin like him. They both laugh and I can see they have a very special bond together. His uncle really cares for Jessy.

We clamber into the plane, take our seats Jessy and Uncle Joe in the front and me in the back with our bags. I remember seeing a plane like this dusting crops back in the states, there are two seats at the front and a bench seat in the back. We all get our seat belts on and Uncle Joe points to ear phones on a hook by the window on my side. I put them on.

As we take off and start to head out, I hear Jessy asking Uncle Joe what's the plan.

"Patience my boy," says his uncle. "first thing first we are heading back to my place in Sydney. Once we land I will explain everything," he adds. Jessy looks over to me and smiles that belter of a smile that makes me relax for the first time in the last week and I begin to trust that it's going to be ok. It's starting to get light now so I can see all around. I spend my time just looking out of the window admiring the scenery.

Its only just over an hour and we land in a field that looks like a makeshift runway, I can see it's been used many times. A barn in the distance that I think Uncle Joe uses for a hangar to store the plane. Then just behind it a beautiful farmhouse. It looks colonial I think to myself. Wooden facade, big windows and a large veranda. Painted white.

Once we have landed and start to slow, I remove the ear phones, we come to a stop just outside the barn. We all get out and Jessy comes to help me with the bags. We head into the house. Uncle Joe tells us to put the bags into the study and Jessy shows me the way.

"You kids hungry?" Uncle Joe shouts out from the kitchen.

"Starving," replies Jessy. We head into the kitchen where Uncle Joe is getting pots out of the cupboard, Jessy heads straight to the fridge and opens it. He grabs a Kabana as his uncle is shaking his head with a loving smile.

With a hint of a giggle in his tone Uncle Joe says, "Hey get outta there, where's your manners ladies first," he tells Jessy. Jessy just smiles and offers me a bite of the Kabana. I giggle and shake my head.

"Uncle Joe," I say to his surprise.

"She speaks!" he says jokingly.

"Is there anywhere I can freshen up, take a shower maybe?"

"Yes of course," he nods his head with understanding. "Jessy show the lady to the upstairs bathroom," he orders Jessy.

Jessy says nothing as he is too busy taking bite after bite of Kabana. Between bites he manages to take a breath, "straight upstairs last door on the left," as he leads me out of the kitchen to the foot of the stairs. He kisses my forehead and returns to the kitchen.

I retrieve my bags from the study and head to the bathroom. A quick shower, freshen up and change of clothes. I feel so much better. The smell of bacon and sausages is coming from the downstairs kitchen and I realise by the loud growling in my stomach that it's been a while since I had eaten and I too am starving. I clear up my thing and head back down to the kitchen bags and all.

"Uncle Joe is cooking one of his 'Famous belly buster'". Jessy explains that this simply means more food than anyone can eat in one sitting.

Uncle Joe asks us to sit at the breakfast bar and he begins to start piling things onto our plates. Rashers of bacon, sausages, beans tomatoes, hash browns, mushrooms and something that Jessy explained was called black pudding! There was so much on the plate I didn't know where to start.

"Tuck in," says Uncle Joe, Jessy needed no encouragement as he was well into his fifth mouthful before I began. Uncle Joe pours us some fresh orange juice and sits with us. I begin to eat I am so hungry I can't eat fast enough. "Crickey" says Uncle Joe,"When did you two last eat?" he asks.

Jessy replies with a mouth full of bacon, "Day before yesterday, I think."

I take one more bite of bacon but can't eat another morsel. I see why it's called a belly buster!

"All done?" asks Uncle Joe. We both nod, and say our thank you. Uncle Joe gets up and gestures for us to follow him as he heads towards his study. It's an old-fashioned room with wood-cladded walls, floor to ceiling book case the full length along one side. An old stately desk like an old-fashioned lawyer's office with a traditional oxblood leather chesterfield sofa opposite. Jessy and I sit on the sofa as Uncle Joe sits behind the desk.

Uncle Joe begins to explain the plan he has for us. "Firstly, new identities untraceable so I am going to get new passports made for you so, I can do that here. This means you will both have new identities known only to me." He continues "Then it's off to Greece. Jessy how is your Greek?," he asks I can see a huge grin all over Jessy's face and I frown not understanding the importance of this.

Jessy turns to me as he can see my confusion, "My grandparents are Greek," he says. "It's a place we visited as a family every year."

Turning back to Uncle Joe who adds, "I have arranged for a charter for you, so you don't have to stay in one place." Uncle

Joe turns to Jessy, "You remember how to sail don't you boy?" he asks.

Jessy's face lights up again, "Yes Uncle." Uncle Joe stands up and presses a button under his desk the bookcase swings into action and one section slides across revealing a steel grey door to another room. As Uncle Joe opens the door it's like a photography studio. Reels of film hanging and trays of liquid, plus a desk and lamp over to one side.

"Very James Bond Uncle," says Jessy and laughs. Uncle Joe just rolls his eyes and shakes his head at the comment. I have no idea what they are talking about.

I turn to Jessy and whisper, "Who's James Bond?" Jessy just shakes his head with a 'I can't believe you just said that' look!

"Come on in," says Uncle Joe.

"Jessy stand over there by that wall please," he adds and Uncle Joe picks up his camera and snaps a photo. "Yes that will do," he says. "You now Hannah," he adds. I move over to the wall and the camera flashes and he takes a photo.

"You need to keep your eyes open love," he say. "Let's try again— Ready?" He gets another picture and says, "That's better we can work with that. You two go and make yourself busy for a couple of hours and I will work on this," says Uncle Joe.

Jessy grabs my hand and we head out of the secret room, through the study back to the front of the farmhouse. "I want to show you something," Jessy tells me with a glint of excitement in his eye.

We head out into the garden and start our way round the side of the farmhouse, it seems partitioned off by high bushes and a couple of trees. We head through an archway and in front of us is a large pool. Jessy starts to take off his clothes and then dives in. He splashes me playfully, "Are you coming in?" he asks. His beaming smile back on his beautiful face.

I can't resist, I bite my bottom lip and feel very brave so I begin to take off my clothes. Jessy starts to swim towards me and sit on the edge of the pool, as he reaches me I lower myself in. Jessy pushes his hair back from his face squeezing away the water running from his hair. He glides over to me and stops nose to nose. I feel his hands touch my waist, and it makes me flinch as it tickles. He slides his hands for a firmer grip around my wait and pulls my hips towards him. He pretends to kiss me and pulls back, he does it again. I smile as it's very arousing, I run my nose along his cheek next to his nose and gently kiss his cheek just catching the edge of his mouth. I do the same on the other side, but Jessy can't hold himself back he starts to kiss me with passion and loses himself in the kiss. I can't get enough of this electricity we have at every touch. Instinctively I open my legs and wrap them around Jessy and I feel a smile on his lips as he kisses me. He kisses and nips at my chin, I tilt my head back as he heads to my neck, I lose control as the sensation is so intense, my hands are running through his hair, caressing him but holding him in place. I feel my hips tilting back and forth instinctively, and Jessy has his hands firmly holding my behind, he moves back slightly adjusting his position.

I feel his erection against me and he speaks gently in my ear, "I don't have a condom."

Through my dreamy state of ecstasy I say, "Its ok."

And before I can blink he has thrust inside me filling me in a ways that sends the most exquisite feeling along my spine to my head, making my back arch and throwing my head back. I open my eyes and pull myself nose to nose with Jessy. He is still inside me, waiting for my approval, I think. I begin to kiss him with all the passion that has built up in me and Jessy does the same. He begins a pace of deep penetration moving in and out with the force of the water matching his movements. His hands are pushing me deeper onto him, his nails digging into my skin. As our bodies continue to build in sensation, he slows the momentum he turns, then moves us both towards the opposite end of the pool, kissing me all the way to the other side, I can see some steps. As we move along the water it's becoming more shallow. My legs tighten around him as we leave the water. Jessy gently kneels and rests me on one of the steps, I can just feel water beneath me. He grabs my legs and hooks his arms under them but holding me firm Jessy, starts once again to pick up pace, my arms are stretch out on both side of me flats against the steps, my chin is pointing up and my head is tilted back my lips parted as each breath lets out a moan of sheer pleasure. The rhythm is so intense I reach my climax and scream out, "YES", a few moment later Jessy reaches his climax and stills. He releases my legs and rests his forehead on my chest.

I stroke his head, as our breathing starts to return to normal and as Jessy lifts his head and pulls out of me, he looks at me caressing my face, "You are so beautiful," he says. "Elly I love you." I have no reply to that hearing those words just makes me happy.

I smile and look at Jessy who smiles that amazing smile back and we lock ourselves in an embrace that is only broken by Uncle Joe shouting awkwardly, "Erm when you're ready, Come to the study." I look at Jessy and he looks at me and we both laugh out loud, in our passion we completely forgot about Uncle Joe!

We enter the study as Uncle Joe requested and it's unclear as to which one of us is more uncomfortable. Neither Jessy or I can look at Uncle Joe.

He hands us over our new passports. Jessy laughs, "Sam Mantalos," he says looking at Uncle Joe, who has a wry smile on his face. "Isn't that the guy we met on our holiday back a couple of years ago— the business man?" Jessy asks.

"I think if I remember," says Uncle Joe, "You had a holiday crush on his daughter." Jessy protests and Jessy and his uncle enter into a debate about their holiday and remembering the good times.

Uncle Joe adds, "All pictures and any connection to these passports have been destroyed," pointing to the ash we can see in the fireplace in his wastepaper bin. I look at mine wondering what wild name I have been given.

"Eleanor Georgiou," I say out loud.

Chapter 17

Greece

A commercial flight into Athens followed by a private charter to a small private airstrip just outside of Argos. Jessy has been telling me all about the South Peloponnese region in Greece where he has visited every year with his family. Telling me all about the Greek islands and his favourite, Rhodes, because of the history there.

A car is waiting for us as we disembark, and we head out towards Nea Kios where the boat charter is waiting for us. On arrival we head into the harbour masters office and he shows us to the boat. Jessy cannot contain his excitement he jumps on board holding out his hand to me to help me up onto the deck.

He shouts back to the harbour master, "Efcharisto Poly," which means thank you. I smile to myself as I'm very impressed with Jessy and his Greek.

The harbour master returns to his office and we both explore the boat. A beautiful fourty-five feet sailing yacht, with a small dingy attached. Kitted with everything from auto pilot to WIFI.

"An Oceanis 45," Jessy says matter of fact. "This is a great boat," he says. "Easy to handle for the two of us, "all mod cons," he says. He is so excited touching buttons, opening cupboards. "Bedroom through that door at the end of the cabin, shower err," he says opening a couple of doors.

"Here," I laugh at him as he so excited but looks so happy too. Uncle Joe has ensured we have all our basic supplies on board with cupboards full of food and drinks.

"Shall we unpack?" I say and Jessy nods. Jessy puts a large envelope on the bed that his Uncle Joe gave to him when he dropped us off at the airport. I ask, "What's in the envelope Jessy."

"Uncle Joe wanted us to have some money to keep us going," he says quickly putting the envelop in a draw next to the bed. As we finish unpacking, Jessy smiles an excited smile and says, "Shall we get this baby on the open water?" he asks. I nod with excitement as I have never been on a sail boat before, but I love the ocean, the waters here of the Aegina Hydra that flow into the Mediterranean are so clear and inviting. Deep turquoise merging into blues gradually darkening to a deep, royal blue with white sand underneath all reflecting the golden sun off the water.

I'm standing next to Jessy as he presses the button that fires up the engine. He looks over at me, smiling that ridiculous smile. A passer-by waves at us and asks if we want him to release the mooring rope.

Jessy tells him, "yes," and he throws it over. I catch it and start to wrap it around my elbow to my hand. Jessy looks at me and looks curious, "you done this before" he asks?

I shake my head, "No."

"Done like a Pro," he shouts back making me smile. The anchor is lifted and I feel the boat start to move, Jessy begins to steer gently moving away from the boardwalk. He starts to add more power from the throttle, and we begin to move into open water out of the harbour.

I sit behind Jessy just watching him as he seems so at ease with piloting the boat, he looks over to me. "Lets head to Santorini," he shouts.

"Sure," I say. We head out, the land behind us of Nea Kios is now out of view. We are on the open water for about two hours we seem to be following a line that mirrors a number of islands, some inhabited as we can see people others look uninhabited. Jessy every so often shouts out the name of the island, as we approach it. Jessy points ahead and explains that's where we are heading. Santorini!

Jessy anchors the boats a little way out as we have the dingy if we need to go ashore.

"Shall I make us something to eat?" I ask.

"That's a good idea," replies Jessy. "Then we can go ashore and explore," he adds.

I smile and head below deck to the kitchen or galley as Jessy corrected me. As I look through the cupboards, I make up my mind to cook some ravioli with a spicy sauce. I quickly make the pasta, and pop it into the fridge whilst I make the filling. As I look in the fridge, I find bacon— I can work with that, mushrooms, garlic and onions. I start merrily chopping and squashing the ingredients. I fry off the bacon to make it crispy and then add the rest in to soak up the flavour. I put half into a bowl and add to the pan some dried chilli flakes and a tin of passata. I find some Worcestershire sauce and slop a few drops of this in too. I dip my finger in and taste for spiciness. Just right! In the cupboard I find a jar of artichokes, So I open this and chop them roughly adding to the bowl. I turn the heat down and gently simmer the sauce.

Jessy shout from top desk, "That smells amazing it's making me hungry."

"Won't be long," I tell him.

I put on a large pan of water for the ravioli. I take the pasta dough out of the fridge and gently push it flat with the heal of my hand. I found a pasta machine in the cupboard. So, I start pressing through the rollers the pasta dough. Once thin enough I cut two strips and fill with the filling I have made, use my finger with some cold water all around the filling ready to seal the two pieces together and put a layer of thin pasta over the filling. Press down with my fingers and the sides of my hands making sure the filling is enclosed. I take a sharp knife and cut around the ravioli. I have made twelve in total six each should be enough, I think to myself. I pop them into the boiling water and cross my fingers they stay sealed, give it a few minutes and then take them out. I have warmed a couple of bowls and place the ravioli in them and scoop over the sauce.

I shout out to Jessy, "It's ready." He comes bounding into the cabin and sits at the table. I pass him the bowl and we sit and eat.

"Wow this is fantastic," Jessy pipes up between mouthfuls. "You are a good cook Elly." "Why thank you kind sir," I say, and we giggle. I clear our plates, and tidy the kitchen. Leaving it all clean for when we return.

I head into the bedroom to get my LV.

Jessy asks, "Where are you going? C'mon lets go."

I smile and say, "I'm getting some cash just in case."

Jessy stops me awkwardly, "I'll get some of the cash Uncle Joe gave us," he says then leads me out to the dingy.

We moor at the harbour and start to explore, but I am conscious of the envelope as Jessy is very weird around it and I start to get a bad feeling.

We stop at a café for coffee and Diples a local desert, then spy a local market with fresh produce. Once we have rested with our coffee we head into the market. Before I know it, we have a couple of bags of fruits and vegetables. It must be late afternoon as the market is closing up and we see less people around us.

"Shall we head back?" Jessy asks. I nod. We arrive back to the boat and Jessy ties the dingy firmly in place then helps me and the bags on to the boat. "You'll get your sea legs soon enough," he says.

I laugh, "What do you mean sea legs?" I say.

"You are still a little wobbly," he adds and we both laugh.

We drop the bags in the cabin below and I say, "Shall we have a swim?"

Jessy looks over to me and replies "Yes, great idea."

We quickly change into swimming clothes. Jessy is changed and out of the cabin before I have found my bikini and I hear a loud splash! I quickly put on my bikini and head out to the top deck, seeing where Jessy is I jump in and splash him. We both laugh and relax enjoying the cool water swimming around the boat. Jessy swims up to me, so I put my arms around him and we tread water nose to nose.

He kisses me, "Are you happy?" he asks.

"Yes Jessy, this is amazing, being here with you, I could never have imagined this in my wildest dreams," I say. He deepens the kiss and we lose ourselves in the passion.

I bite my bottom lip and start to head back to the boat, I clamber up the steps and start to remove my bikini showing Jessy exactly what he is missing. He responds by following me on board.

We start to kiss and head below deck both of us banging our heads and elbows as the space below is not designed for two people in passionate embraces. We burst into the bedroom. Jessy turns me round and presses my back into his front. He kisses and nips at my shoulders, I oblige by tilting my head to one side, he starts to kiss my neck. His arm is holding me firmly against him, one hand caressing my breast and the other between my legs, he inserts his finger and groans, followed by a thrust of his penis inside me.

I lean forward and outstretch my arms to the bed as the sensation instantly electric. Jessy takes both hands onto my hips and begins a pace of hard thrusts followed by slowly moving back to position for another thrust, its exquisite and I moan loudly, Jessy leans forward and he kissing my back gently moving in and out. His hand moves forward to my clitoris and he begins a combination on circling my clitoris and moving in and out of me filling me with so much sensation I am not sure I can handle.

His pace begins to quicken and I am overwhelmed with all the electricity flowing through my whole body, my legs begin to stiffen and Jessy is breathing heavy through gritted teeth, I can't hold on any more I scream out, "YES, YES, YEEEAAS," and Jessy explodes inside me. He catches me with his strong arms as my legs give way from so much pleasure. We flop onto the bed together and allow our breathing to return to normal.

It's been such a hectic couple of days I can't say I know what day it is anymore, but what I do know is I am exhausted. I can't keep my eyes open and I drift into s deep but contented sleep.

When I wake, I rise up onto my elbows and see that I am alone, the bed is messy and I can see that Jessy has been in bed next to me. I jump up and try to see if I can see Jessy. He's not in the cabin he must be on deck.

I can't help myself I have to see what is in the envelope that Uncle Joe gave to Jessy.

I slowly and carefully trying not to make any noise open the draw and take out the envelope. As I look inside there is money, a lot! A phone, a dossier and more passports. I take everything out except the money. I am drawn to the passports first and see that both Jessy and I have another three identities each. The phone looks just like the one from before so I assume it's for emergencies. Then I pick up the dossier. As I open it, I can see a picture of me.

"What the hell is this?" I say out loud. I take the photo out and start to work my way through the files, firstly, it's a missing person's report that was filed by my dad. Then there is an CIA document detailing the institute and listing 311y as a test subject. There are transcripts from a number of interviews where I have helped with information. I start to shake as I see a photo and the escape report. The report is my mother's shooting and there is a picture of her lying on the ground shot! I start to cry this is too much. I carry on trying to wipe away the tears and I see three reports one at aged five, one when I was ten and the last when I was fifteen all detailing the advancement of my abilities. I hear a noise from on deck and quickly put everything back in order back into the envelop and firmly back in the draw.

I wipe my eyes hoping it can't be noticed as I need to process what I have just read. How did Uncle Joe get this information, why has he given it to Jessy, has the recovery team been notified of where I am? So many questions and I can't read his memories to know for sure.

One thing though I do know for sure is that I am coming up to my twentieth birthday which means that based on the timeline so far my abilities will evolve.

Chapter 18

A Mothers Love

Joe suddenly appears in my room, it makes me jump as it was unexpected. He is followed by my mum. "We have only about ten minutes before they notice the surveillance cameras are off."

"Elly please don't ask questions, I need to see into Joe's memories," Mum says. "I need to obtain his contacts for getting you out of here," she adds. I gasp in surprise and look scared. She holds my hand and says, "Don't worry, I will never let anyone hurt you ever again."

Joe comes over and sits on the bed. He holds out his hand. We make a connection, I go back to my birthday and the incident. It's like I am looking through images in a book. Pictures, and I hear the voices of the dialogue and what is being said. I also feel the same emotions, from angry to scared. The levels of scared range from a slight worried feeling scared of being caught out to terrified, scared of being killed as many have before.

I see an image of Joel, then Cassie I see a woman and Cassie smiling saying thank you. I try to go back more. Its blocked somehow like a door that is locked and I can't open.

I can only see this woman, I ask myself who is she, what is her role in this. I say it two or three times in my mind before Joe answers, "It's my sister Deb."

I look at my mum and she looks at me then Joe, "What just happened?" mum says.

"I was asking who is the woman helping Cassie," I explain. Joe frowns as he is not sure what's happening.

I close my eyes and start to bring Joe back to now, as I don't want to affect any of his memories. But I stop. I see Joe entering a room with the Director and the General. My dad is there but not my mum. I focus in on this.

"I want her in Cuba," says the General. "It's time, this has been her purpose since she was created," he continued.

"But she is only fifteen," adds Tom. "It's only been six months, she needs more time to adapt to the new abilities."

"I am not wasting any more time and resources," replies the General with a steely glare over to the Director.

"I have to agree with the General, Tom," says the director all sheepish.

Tom pleads, "let me do more tests, over the next couple of weeks and then by the end of the month she should be ready," he adds desperately. "Another three weeks that's all" he pleads. "We have been down this road before with some of the other subjects and we have failed as we pushed too early and they could not control their abilities." He continues, "Elly has proved from the very first cell divide she is unique."

The General looks over to the Director. For guidance. The Director turns to the General and adds, "It can only reinforce her ability if we can study her further," Trying to not be intimidated by the General. The General looks very annoyed.

He turns to the both of them and says, "One week then we are transferring her to Cuba."

I release Joe and say out loud, "I don't want to go." Joe and Mum look at each other.

"Its ok Elly that's why we are here," Mum adds trying to reassure me. "We are going to get you out before that can happen!" "Joe, we need to contact your sister," Mum says frantically. Joe Nods. "Elly do you want some tea monkey?" Mum asks trying to calm the situation and ease the tension. "I'll get some and be right back" She adds. Both her and Joe leave the room.

Mum returns with tea and biscuits and sits on the bed. It's a little bit of normal as we do this every day. She is behaving strangely though compared to when she was in here before. I ask, "Is everything ok?"

She replies, "Yes darling of course," but points to a note on the tray.

It reads:

Don't react but the cameras are back on and they can see and hear everything we say.

I sip my tea and say nothing. We finish our tea in silence and mum takes out the tray, she passes Oscar at the door who is coming in with my lunch. Oscar asks if she would like him to take the tea tray and mum smiles and lets him know its ok she can manage.

I notice on the lunch tray the napkin has some writing on it, it reads:

Tonight at 5pm, be ready.

I finish my lunch and use the napkin to wipe the tray where there is any moisture to try and make the napkin soggy and dissolve the message. I am now on edge, what do I do? I head into the bathroom and stare at the mirror, I see my whole body shaking as I have no idea what to expect. I'm scared what is going to happen.

It's getting close to 5pm. Mum comes into the room and says, "Elly can you be in the lab in five minutes please." I nod and get myself up, as this must be it! I think to myself.

I enter the lab and Joe is there, he hands me a Louis Vuitton small bag. "There is money, change of identity and instructions in here for you to leave the US."

I put the bag over one arm and it rests across my chest. The panic inside me is not allowing me to speak. I nod at Joe so that he sees I understand. He tells me to put on the coat he has brought in and hat, I do so quickly without question. Mum appears at the exit door to the lab, I have no idea what is on the other side as I have never been through there.

She turns to Joe and me and says, "It's now or never" .

I stop myself for just a second to take stock of my thoughts and actions, calming my mind.

As we exit the lab into the main area, Joe leaves by the door to my bedroom.

As I look both ways to the corridor, I see at each end white coats rushing, hurried in their movements some carrying medical supplies and then I see others with guns.

I hear a strange sound in the distance, that resonates from my bedroom and it sounds like a gunshot. Then a siren sounds, I think to myself, Oh no, Joe!. I just want to see what's going on, as I sense something not good. We take the left-hand side corridor and slowly hugging the wall make our way to the end. As I sneakily look around the corner, I can see the orderly's station, manned by people with guns. Plus, the kitchen is opposite. But why? what's going on.

Mum looks back at me and says, "Don't look OK." I can't resist the nosey urge and have to look. As we get closer, I see blood, lots of it. Fear is creeping over me as I have never seen so much before. I can sense a tragedy, wrongdoing and pain. But I don't know what it means.

We move slowly towards to station; all the focus is ahead of me, so no one is paying any attention to me. I reach one of the white coats and peer through the gap, its Joe lying on the floor with a single bullet to the head, his eyes wide open. I can see the Director heading towards the commotion and then my dad is kneeling by Joe closing his eyes. He stops and lowers his head for a moment, then turns to the Director and says he's gone. Mum is pulling me into the kitchen as this is the distraction she can use.

As my dad looks up, he can see me through the gap entering the kitchen.

"Elly," he says without thinking and everyone turns towards me especially the director. We now panic and run.

I hear shouting behind me. "Stop!"

We head into the outside, its dusk. A car is right in front of us.

"Get in," Mum shouts frantically, a loud bang rings out and then it all goes quiet. "You have to go," mum says strained. "Put this button in D" as she points to the automatic gears, and press hard this pedal. Another loud bang the last thing she said to me was, "Don't look back monkey, keep running and never reveal to anyone what you can do. Trust no-one." She pulls her locket off her neck as hands it to me. Then she was gone.

As I look around I see that my dad has his arm stretched out and a gun pointing towards us. He shot her, he killed her. I scream out, "NO!" as she is no longer breathing.

With steely determination and floods of tears streaming down my face, I jump into the driving seat of the car, I turn the key and put the car in "D." I press the pedal but I don't move. I panic and start pressing buttons as guards and my dad are running towards me. Suddenly the car surges forward. I push the pedal flat to the floor and steer the car for my life depends upon it. I have no idea where I am going or even how to stop this car. I head towards a gate and see more guards, I just carry on I can hear the cars behind me and try to take a quick look and the car swerves as I turn around. Mirroring the movement of my as my hands are on the steering wheel.

"Stupid," I say out loud to myself. I crash through the security barrier and gates hearing shots being fired at the car. Ahead I can see nothing but desert. Where the heck am I?

Luckily the road is straight, I am driving at 160km it reads on the dashboard. There are several vehicles behind me. Catching up with me. My tears are blurring my vision and I keep swerving as I take a hand off the wheel to keep wiping my tears. There is a big truck ahead and I swerve to pass it losing control of the vehicle, I veer off the road onto the dirt and clouds of dust fly up. I haven't released the pedal and am still at 160km. I pass the truck and head back onto the road misjudging the distance and cutting in front of the truck. This makes the truck swerve to avoid hitting me, it jack-knifes and with the dust clouds, the chasing cars crash into the big truck. I just keep going and stop for nothing. After about an hour or so I see ahead in the distance a rest stop. A big sign high up saying 'GAS'. The car begins to judder, I have no idea what's happening. I continue with my foot on the pedal pressed as far down as possible. I am slowing down. As I reach the rest stop the car is almost to a stop I turn in and just let it come to a stop.

I see someone approaching the car and panic, It's dark and I can't make out who it is. As they come closer, I can see that its Deb, Joe's sister. How is she here?

"Elly!" I hear a voice shout. It makes me jump, but I think she is here to help. I open the car door and jump out.

"I'm here" I respond.

"Thank goodness, are you ok?" she asks.

"I think so," I reply.

"Where is Susan?" She asks I begin to sob. "Oh no," she says and puts her arms around me to comfort me. "We need to move on," she adds quietly. "I have everything you need in the car, C'mon let's get going," she says reassuringly.

I get into her car and we head out. I watch her operate the car it seems pretty simple. We chat a little about me driving the car in the escape and I ask why it was stuck. She explained to me about the hand brake. I just think to myself one of the buttons must have released it. As we continue the drive, I am exhausted and can't keep my eyes open I drift off to sleep.

The bleeping is getting louder, louder almost defining. A clunking sound and a backfire reign out. I gasp and bolt upright and am sitting in the car, we have stopped. I am sweating, racing heart, breathing fast and trying to look around for anything familiar. I remember now as I start to calm, I am with Deb, but where is she? The beeping is still loud, and I look all around to see where the noise is coming from its a waste collection truck reversing. I am at another rest stop. I see Deb in the window. I sit back and Deb comes back to the car.

"Morning Sleepy head" she says. "I needed to stop for Gas, hungry?" she asks. I nod. She hands me over a bag. I can feel the warmth from it. As I open it, I can see coffee and doughnuts!

"Where are we?" I ask.

"We are not far now from Bakersfield," Deb explains. We are heading to LA as we have you booked on a scheduled commercial flight to Hawaii.

Chapter 19

The Envelope Revealed

It's always the same, a new place and more of my memories keep surfacing as new memories that I make are triggering old ones I have tried to forget.

"Elly, wake up, Elly can you hear me?" Jessy is shaking me to bring me out of my flashback. As I come too, I am so very sad. "What?" I say instinctively to Jessy.

"You were dreaming again," he says. "The same as before."

I look down at my hands and holding back tears I tell him, "It's the day my mother was killed, and how I escaped," I explain.

"Tell me about it," he replies. "It might help," he smiles and gently tucks my hair around my ear.

As I look up at him, I ask, "Why do you have a dossier on me from the CIA?" Jessy freezes, looks shocked. "I looked inside the envelope as you were acting all weird," I tell him.

He straightens himself up and runs a hand through his hair. Scratching the back of his head, searching his thoughts to find the right words to respond with. He knows this is critical."OK," he says. "Don't freak out. I honestly didn't know anything about this until we headed to Sydney Airport. Uncle Joe only mentioned it then," he continues. "He was worried about me and wanted to check you out."

"But how did he get these files, they are from the Institute?" I ask.

"I honestly don't know," Jessy explains. "I can only assume it's through his M16 connections." He shrugs and shakes his head as he genuinely has no idea.

"If he has these files, he is now in serious danger," I add. "These are from the Institute and they now have another lead."

Jessy shifts uncomfortable and looks really worried, he replies, "Uncle Joe is careful and he can look after himself." But as I look at him I think this is more to convince himself that his uncle will be ok.

"Jessy, we have to have a plan," I say. "If we are tracked here what are our options." Jessy nods in agreement. He reaches into the draw and takes out the envelope.

"Have you read it?" I ask.

"No, I haven't had chance, Uncle Joe explains what was in it."

I put the dossier to one side, we count the money in the envelop ten thousand Euro, plus we have ten thousand Australian Dollars from Pamela and the three thousand I have saved. We look at the passports. "So, we have a Greek passport the ones we used to enter Greece. A new Australian passport each and Canadian" I listed to Jessy. I also remembered I have an American Passport that Deb gave me that I decided to keep to myself.

"How safe do you think these identities are?" I ask Jessy.

"Its M16," he says. "Spy stuff. Uncle Joe said he is the only person who knows the identities."

I sigh some relief and say out loud, "Yes, I think we might be ok as Uncle Joe showed us that he had destroyed our photos."

Jessy nods and strokes my hand. "We will be ok," he says reassuringly.

"I'm starving," Jessy pipe us changing the subject.

I can't help but smile and let out a giggle, "Me too," I say. Let's get something to eat. We leave everything on the bed and head into the galley.

Jessy springs into action looking at our supplies. "How about a bacon sandwich?" he asks.

"Sure, sounds good," I say. Jessy promptly gets on with making our breakfast using the fresh bread we bought at the market the day before. The smell is very appetizing and making my stomach growl. It seems to be ready in a flash and I pour us a glass of fresh orange juice each and we tuck in.

"Shall we go fishing today?" Jessy asks. "We can catch some fish and BBQ," he explains.

"Erm ok," I say. "I have no idea how to catch fish," I add.

Jessy laughs out loud, "I will teach you," he says.

Once we have eaten, we head back into the bedroom to get ready, still having everything spread across the bed. We both eye the dossier but awkwardly ignore it. We head out on deck. Jessy has found some snorkel gear and a harpoon. He merrily explains what we do with the snorkel gear and advises that he will take charge of the harpoon. I nod in agreement as I'm fearful I would shoot Jessy accidentally.

He must of seen my appreciation of his control of the harpoon and says out loud, "I would hate for you to shoot me accidentally."

I laugh out loud and say, "Oh my god I was just thinking that, you read my mind." We laugh together and seem once again at ease with each other.

The majority of the day is spent in the water fishing, swimming and just enjoying each other's company. We don't head out too far from the boat and keep it in sight. We are not very good at fishing as hours go by and still no fish for the BBQ. We decide to head back onto the boat and enjoy the suns heat, drying off quickly. Every so often a passing boat waves and we wave back. Santorini is quite a busy place, there are a lot of visitors it appears. We both sit on the deck enjoying the sun, Jessy asks if I am hungry. I nod and he heads into the galley below deck. He appears a short while later with wine and a board full of cheese, salami, grapes, sundried tomatoes and Bread.

"Oh, what's this?" I ask.

"Antipasti," he says matter of fact.

We tuck in and spend the rest of the day eating, drinking wine, talking about Jessy's holiday experiences with his family. Every now and again Jessy slips into a reverie thinking about his mum and sister's I guess. Before we know where we are its dusk and Jessy is lighting the boat lights on deck as the light is dimming.

"I have had such a great day," I tell Jessy.

He smiles and kisses my nose. "Me too" he says.

He takes all of our things back into the galley and come back on deck. We carry on talking Jessy explaining the first time his dad took him sailing on one of their trips to Crete and another time him and his dad went fishing whilst they holidayed in Rhodes and caught so much fish that they gave a local restaurant some. I assumed it was his mum and sister's he was missing but the way he talks about his dad I hear torment in his voice. It's such a wonder to hear all the amazing things Jessy and his family did, as for me I have never had an experience anything like that.

In the distance we can see the lights of Santorini and its beautiful like fireworks as there are different coloured lights on and off occasionally,

Jessy leans over and puts his arm around me, "Are you cold?" he asks.

"Yes a little," I say.

He heads into the cabin I think its to get a jumper for me. I watch as he enters the bedroom he sees all the things from that envelope still spread out on the bed. His eyes go straight to the dossier.

He picks up one of his jumpers and the dossier and head up onto the deck.

He hands me the jumper and asks, "can I read this?" I nod and put the jumper on.

I try and gauge the reactions looking at each micro movement on his face. But I can't read him at all. Every so often he seems uncomfortable and his hand runs through his hair, he looks over to me and smiles a half smile.

"What are you thinking?" I ask.

"The things you have gone through," he adds. "It makes me so angry that someone could hurt you like that," he says gently.

As he reads the reports on my abilities, he suddenly closes the dossier and says. "Elly your twentieth birthday is only two weeks away."

Chapter 20

Twenty

I am shocked as it's the day before my birthday and I feel ok. Usually I am unwell on the lead up to it. But this time is different. Jessy is constantly fussing round me asking if I am ok. It's getting quite annoying.

The last couple of weeks have been spent pretty much on the boat we have travelled from Santorini down to Crete and moored in the harbour at Heraklion. We needed to refuel and replenished some of our supplies.

We have spent a lot of time site seeing with Jessy telling me all about his trips to these places and what he remembers. It's funny as some places have changed quite a lot and he gets quite confused but tries to make out it's what we remembers saying.

"Oh yes that's it I remember now." Which makes me laugh as he is covering up what he has forgotten. But I'm sure from the stories that Jessy has been telling me of are from a considerable time ago when he was fifteen years old.

We are sitting at a café having breakfast, and there is a silence between us not from eating but caused from being

161

anxious of what is going to happen in the next twenty four hours.

The last couple of weeks have been so relaxed that I try to take the mood back to that. "So Jessy, tell me about your last trip with your family."

He smiles as he recalls the happy times. "My Uncle Joe came on that trip," he recalls. "As a coincidence it was also in Crete," he says. "Dad was a little distracted as he had just won this major contract with a new client, Cayman Industries and he wanted to make sure everything was handled properly. He told us it was worth a lot of money to the family business. "Oh and I remember," he adds excitedly, "Do you remember Uncle Joe teasing me about the new name he has given me?" he asks me.

"Yes, I remember the businessman's daughter crush," I say teasing him.

"Yeah that's the one," he replies sarcastically. "Whilst we were on our holiday, the businessman turns up out of the blue and speaks to my dad. I don't think dad was happy as he seemed awkward, a little wary or on edge, But then ends up spending a couple of days with us," Jessy says with a curious tone and shrugs his shoulder. He thinks nothing more of it and continues the story of this last vacation.

We head back to the boat walking hand in hand enjoying the sun and heat, trying to view all the whitewashed buildings that are all around us but pretty much blinded from the suns reflection of them. We can see small café's and some bars plus small side streets leading to the unknown. People sat in front of their doors chatting to neighbours.

"It's really beautiful here," I say to Jessy and he smiles and nods back in agreement. Everyone we walk past smiles and nods a greeting and we both smile back. As we reach the boat I turn to Jessy "I'm feeling a little dizzy," and before I know it I have passed out. The last thing I remember is Jessy crying out, "Elly."

I start to stir and realise that I am not on the boat. As I squint and try to focus there are lots of beeping noises all around me. I can see Jessy at the side of the bed he is asleep, his head on the bed and holding my hand. I move my hand and he stirs. He realises that I am awake and shouts, "Nurse she is awake, Nurse." He stands frantically and strokes my forehead gently, smiling in relief it seems.

A woman appears in a white coat, Goddard on a name badge. Young maybe in her late twenties tanned skin, blonde and blue eyes really quite pretty. She reminds me of the institute and how she is dressed, and I tense up, looking around trying to get a sense of where I am. "It's ok," she says. "Your safe," she adds. "I need to check you over," she says flashing lights in my eyes making me squint and lift my hand up to cover my eyes.

Jessy tries to help by stopping me move my hands, "Its ok Elly she a friend." he tells me.

I shrug my hand out of his and try to sit up. She stops me and say, "No you need to stay still." she presses a button and a two more people come into the room. Followed by Uncle Joe. The two men position themselves either side of me and are holding gently my shoulders to keep me lying down.

"We are not trying to hurt you Elly, but you have been in a coma for the last four weeks. We need to make sure that everything is ok." She explains.

I look over to Jessy and wonder where I am and why Uncle Joe is here. Jessy suddenly stands up. With everyone turning around startled by his sudden movement, "What did you say?" he says out loud shocked.

I look at him and frown I say again in my mind, "Did you hear me?" I look over to him and he nods.

"Uncle Joe, I heard Elly in my mind," Jessy explains to Uncle Joe. "She spoke to me in my head," he adds with horror. "Am I going mad?" he says.

Uncle Joe laughs. "NO Son, you're not," he replies. "This must be the next evolution of her abilities," he explains.

I close my eyes and drift in and out of consciousness. I sense a lot of people coming in and out of the room and I only catch fragments of conversation. Mostly Uncle Joe and Jessy. Jessy asking Uncle Joe what's happening and am I going to be ok.

I wake again and the room is empty. I scan the room for exits. I can see a camera in the ceiling that must cover the whole room and only one door as a way in and out of the room, that I recall everyone using from before. I continue to look around noticing the monitors beeping and I can see a tube going to my arm. I pull out the needle removing the tube and whatever liquid is in there. Alarms sound and in comes the blonde again.

"We need to put this back," she says.

I look at her.

"No," I say out loud. She stops freezes on the spot. I look at her and stare directly into her eyes. I can see her thoughts. How am I doing this without touch I ask myself? I can see she works for the British Army, we are in a US Naval base in Crete – Souda Bay. I think to myself its odd but then I see as a medic she is part of a joint operation with service personnel from all different military countries.

I am searching for when I first came into the hospital. Jessy is accompanied by Uncle Joe who is talking frantically on the phone. But I can't make out what he is saying. They are greeted by MP's who show them to the room I am in. Dr Goddard enters enters seeing me for the first time. She nods to Uncle Joe, she knows him from somewhere.

"Help her Terry," Uncle Joe pleads. ^

"You need to go to the waiting area and let me look at her," she tells Uncle Joe.

More people enter the room helping assist Dr Goddard with diagnosis. Uncle Joe and Jessy head out to wait. Lots of activity and people are plugging in monitors, taking blood, setting up drip lines. After about an hour she goes to find Uncle Joe.

"All I can tell you at this stage is, she is in a coma, her brain has swollen and we can't see any reason for this such as trauma or infection," she explains. "We have taken some blood samples and will test and see what comes back," she smiles and explains further "It's going to be a long night but we will keep an eye on her."

Jessy sighs and is holding back tears, Uncle Joe comforts him. "She's in good hands son," he says and nods his appreciation to Dr Goddard before she leaves the room.

I blink and Dr Goddard looks frightened.

"What just happened?" she says. "I couldn't move," She adds. "Who are you Elly?"

I grab her hand and smile. "It's ok, I'm not a threat to you," I tell her gently. I ask, "Who knows I am here?."

She looks puzzled. "No-one," she replies.

"How do you know Joe?" I ask.

"We have worked together for the last three years," she explains.

"So you are M16 too?" I ask.

She frowns and shakes her head, "No Army!"

I release her hand and she steps back. I close my eyes and begin to explain. "Dr Goddard," I say. "Please listen, let me explain. I would never cause you harm, please do not be afraid of me." I continue, "I am only twenty-years old and have been hunted for the last four years by the division of a government agency. My mother was shot in front of me," and I picture my mum lying there by the car. "She died trying to help me escape from the clutches of the same government you work for. I have been treated as a lab rat my whole life." I picture lab test with convicts, and my dad hitting me with his fist and belt. I hear her gasp with horror. I open my eyes and realise that I have transferred my thoughts to her.

"Oh my god," she cries out.

"Please help me," I ask out loud.

She comes over to my bed and grabs my hand. "What do you need?" she asks.

"Please make sure there are no records, or traces of me in this facility," I say. "Destroy blood samples everything that links to me regardless of what name its under." She nods squeezes my hand and hurries out of the room.

I lay back on the bed as feel exhausted, I have realised that my abilities have evolved I now have the ability to transfer my thoughts, speak telepathically, control others by my mind and I don't need a touch to make a connection.

I drift into a daydream all burry at first then as my mind vision sharpens, I see the Veritas strike team! They are landing at Crete International Airport. I can see them disembarking and heading into two black pimped up vehicles. The same I remember from before, they were waiting for them on the tarmac. I can see a dossier held by one and he opens it to advise the driver where to head out to. They are coming here! I notice the same man look at his watch and it says 20:30pm. I pull out of the daydream and look up to see a clock on the wall. Its 14:30am what did I just see! I ask myself.

Can I see the future?

I start to get dressed.

Jessy appears. "Whats going on?" he asks.

"We need to go NOW!" I say.

"You need to rest," he adds. I grab his hand and show him the vision.

When I release him, he looks at the clock and replies, "OK." We head out and Uncle Joe is waiting. "Don't ask," Jessy pipes up. "We need to go now to the boat."

Uncle Joe searches Jessy's face for some reason and can see the fear, so does as he is asked.

A car takes us back to the boat and we say our hurried goodbyes to Uncle Joe. As we see Uncle Joe heading out of sight, we start up the boat. Nothing. Jessy looks at me as I am throwing back the mooring ropes.

"What wrong?" I shout.

"Not sure but the boat won't start," he replies. Suddenly Jessy leaps into action and smiles saying, "Old School it is."

Looking puzzled as I have no idea what's going on I say, "What?"

Jessy laughs and as he does he lowers the main sail. We begin to drift out of the harbour and suddenly the sail crack and fills as we start to pick up pace. We have only an hour before the Veritas team arrive into Crete. We head out to Sea.

Acknowledgements

This book is a testament to the most amazing support of Emily Whitehead with her guidance, and pushing me to do better. Plus, all her encouragement all the way through, which has given a novice such as myself the confidence to believe in what can be achieved. Also to Busybird Publishing that again have been an absolute gem in supporting an emerging author to realise a dream come true. You are so amazing!

A heartfelt thank you to my dearest friends Debbie Reid, Diane Page, Sam Matandos, Gary Jackson and Steve Failla who from the outset not only congratulated me but never seemed shocked at my announcement of publishing a novel. You gave me the confidence to make it happen.

And finally, to my family Alex, Danny, Nadine, Ashleigh, Tom and Thomas with my wonderful grandchildren Summer, Olivia, Esme and Alfie you are my absolute world and I love you all to the moon and back.

About the Author

Pamela Dabbs was born in Leicestershire in the UK. Journeyed through a working career of operational bias management that culminated with her last employment being asked if she would take up a position in Melbourne, Australia.

A firm believer in seizing opportunities that present themselves, Pamela packed up her life with her Husband Nick, two Dogs – Mr. Gibbs and Willow – and travelled to Australia in February of 2019.

In awe of the country, its most amazingly warm-hearted people, and of course the coffee culture, in Melbourne has been a place that feels like it was always home. With also a relaxed way of life enabling the dreams to become a reality and put pen to paper in this new series of books.

Coming Soon

Book 2 – *The Sanctum*

A deep look into the project that created Elly and what happens next with Jessy and Uncle Joe. Leaving Greece and the Islands to go to Europe. What Elly discovers here will change her life forever.